TRICKY
BUSINESS

TRICKY BUSINESS

Cathie Bartlam

Scripture Union

130 City Road, London EC1V 2NJ

By the same author
Go for Gold – *Leopard Book*
Operation Sandy – *Tiger Book*

© Cathie Bartlam 1990
First published 1990

ISBN 0 86201 605 3

Phototypeset by Input Typesetting Ltd, London
Printed and bound in Great Britain by
Cox and Wyman Ltd, Reading.

1

'Come on, you wimps, we can do it. Don't you dare chicken out now!' Sal whispered across to a reluctant Narrinder while Tag and Cowboy muttered their protests.

'We'll get into trouble,' protested Tag, trying to bite his nails at the same time as holding his bag of stones.

'Don't be a wet,' hissed Sal. 'We all agreed. Just hurry up. Break is nearly over.'

The four ten year olds crept into the cloakroom and over to the wire basket full of lunch-boxes.

'Whose shall we do?' asked Cowboy, who always made a lot of noise and fuss, but did not seem to have any ideas in his head.

'Anyone's. Just grab the nearest. Like this.' Sal demonstrated. She pulled out the boxes, emptied the sandwiches and cake onto the floor and replaced them with a pile of stones. The others copied her. Well, they always did. Everyone knew that Sal was the leader of the gang.

Nearby a door slammed.

'Out! Get out!' said Sal, gathering the food up. 'Chuck this lot in the bins.'

Quickly they escaped back to the playground, their anoraks bulging with the food. As casually as they could, they walked over to the bins. Ah, good. Mr Page, the teacher on duty, was not watching. Yet another baby first-year had fallen over and was crying. That would keep old Page occupied.

Disposing of the food quietly, the four went across to where the rest of 3N were playing, just as old Page rang the bell. Getting into line Sal winked at Narrinder. She could not wait until dinner time. What a laugh it would be when they fetched their lunch-boxes. She especially wanted to see Vicki's face. Well, it was her own fault, bringing chicken portions or individual pies for *her* lunch. Sandwiches were good enough for the rest of them but not for her, it seemed.

Narrinder did not return the wink. She was a bit scared. One day she would tell Sal what she thought of some of her tricks. But not yet. If she did Sal might not be her friend and it was bad enough being the only Asian girl in the class, without losing her friends as well.

At last the morning's lessons finished. The lunch bell rang and the usual stampede for the cloakroom began.

'Those having dinners, line up. Those on sandwiches, wait!' screeched Miss Winter above the din. She yelled the same words every day at twelve o'clock, but no one took much notice. Except today. Sal and her friends did not seem to be in such a hurry.

As Miss Winter escaped to the safety of the staff-room, chaos broke out in the cloakroom.

'Where's my box?'

'What the. . . . ?'

'Hey, who did this?'

'Where's my crisps . . . and chocolate cake?'

Some of the children looked on bewildered. Their food was safe. What was all the fuss about?

'Mummy did me garlic bread and French cheese,' whined Vicki. 'Now it's all gone.'

Garlic bread indeed, thought Sal. Who did Vicki think she was? All the racket brought out the dinner-ladies who 'tut-tutted' and tried to restore order. Miss Winter was sent for and when she arrived there was instant calm.

'Right then,' she boomed, weighing up the situation in a split second, 'Who is responsible for this?'

No one, it seemed.

'Well, we will just stay here until the culprit owns up.' Miss Winter was onto a loser, thought Sal. Tag and Cowboy had disappeared to have dinners and Narrinder would never tell on her. Sal knew from experience that she could put on her best smile, look angelic and lie like mad all at the same time.

The teacher questioned each child, getting, 'No' from everyone. She had her suspicions. Odd things were always happening in her class. This was just the latest, and silliest. The trouble was that Miss Winter could never get proof of who was behind these escapades. She felt that Sal knew more about them than she let on. However getting her, or anyone else, to admit that had, so far, been impossible.

She looked at Sal particularly closely and asked, 'Are you sure, Sal, that you've had nothing to do with this?'

'Me, Miss! Of course not.' Sal's green eyes gazed up innocently, at the same time as she scuffed her worn trainers on the floor. There was nothing to be done except to let the class go. Cook said that she would find a few left-overs for those with stones for lunch.

In the playground everyone was talking about the mystery of 3N's lunch-boxes. Who would have dared to do it?

'Look, Sal,' said Tag. 'Perhaps we'd better not do any tricks for a bit.'

'Why not? We said we would always be a tricks gang.'

'Well, can't we just be a gang for playing, for a bit anyway?' asked Tag.

'Yes, can't we?' echoed Cowboy, twisting his check shirt round in his hands. He always wore it, which is why the others called him Cowboy.

'Please,' Narrinder joined in. 'We nearly got caught then.' Sal looked at them. They were pathetic. Tag, a great big lad, clothes straining at the seams, was biting what was left of his nails and seemed near to tears. Cowboy was agreeing with the others and Narrinder, pretty, neat Narrinder, looked scared. Why couldn't they all have a good laugh about it together? The plan had worked, hadn't it?

'We won't have any fun, then,' began Sal. 'Scaredy-cats.' She stopped. If she did not agree then they might not want to be in her gang. She might be left with no gang at all! Perhaps it would be better to forget tricks for a while. Anyway it was getting harder to think them up. She hadn't been sure that this last one would work.

'Okay. No tricks for a bit. Come on, let's play football.' Off they went to join in with some of their other friends.

All afternoon Sal felt as if Miss Winter was watching her. As if she knew . . . but she couldn't really. Sal fiddled with her hair during the lessons until her wispy ginger bunches had come loose completely and her face was smeared with ink. The blue blobs merged with her sprinkled freckles and the stain of tomato sauce left over from her lunch. Sal did not care. She always looked a mess. She wished she was a boy and then no one would expect her to be clean all the time. Mum was getting fed up with washing her clothes every day. Still that was Mum's problem.

Usually Miss Winter read 3N a book at the end of school, but today was different.

'I want to tell you about a competition,' she said. 'Now settle down and be quiet. This is a competition with prizes!' A sort of hush spread over the fidgeting class.

'In three weeks' time we break up for Easter.' Miss Winter paused for all the 'hoorays' and cheers to stop.

'I want you all to do an Easter project. It's got to be mounted on a piece of card or paper so we can put them all on the wall. It can be anything at all to do with Easter. The first prize of a large chocolate egg will go to the person who is the most creative, who has the most original ideas.'

Miss Winter droned on with lots of ideas about Easter, but Sal was not listening. I'll do the best Easter project, she thought, then Miss Winter will like me and will forget about the lunch-boxes. If I do a really good project she will be sure to think I'm not to blame. I'll do something amazing and I'll start tonight.

2

Sal dashed into the house.

'Hello. It's me. I've got to do a project. Now.'

There was no response. Sal went into the living-room. Mum was lying flat out on the floor while Sal's little sister Lizzie crawled over her. Two other small children were sitting, glued to the television set. Cartoons again. And an older boy, about six, was trying to jam crayons into the cassette player.

'Hey, Mum, I said, I've got to do a project.'

Mum heaved herself upright. Being a child-minder was no picnic and she was tired. Another two hours until the last child would be picked up.

She turned to listen, brushing pieces of Lego off her jumper. She always wore jeans and jumpers. Today she was wearing the one with the polar bear on. He was rather grubby by now but Mum did not notice. Picking up a hairbrush that was conveniently on top of the fire-place, she made a good job of tidying up the thick black curly hair that framed her long half smiling face.

'Oh, hello, Sal,' she said. 'Will you change Lizzie's nappy while I get Paul out of the cassette player?'

Sal automatically changed the nappy, throwing the soiled one into the kitchen bin, although it was supposed to go in the dustbin outside. Lizzie was quite cute really, with her beaming smile and chubby pink legs. Sal sent her out of the kitchen and put the kettle on.

'Make you a cup of tea,' she shouted, 'and one for "Them".'

'Them' were Boss and Grump, her older brothers who were fifteen and fourteen. They would cycle in from school soon. She chuckled. Time for a bit of fun.

She had just got the mugs out and the teapot ready, when Mum came in and slumped at the kitchen table.

'That Paul is the worst,' she said. 'Thank goodness I only have him after school. I think they'll all watch TV for a bit now. Pour us a cuppa, there's a good girl.'

Just then the back door flew open. Boss charged in followed by Grump.

'I'm starving,' yelled Boss, opening the cupboard door. 'Where's the chocolate spread?'

'Do me one,' demanded Grump, throwing his filthy rugby kit onto the floor. 'I'm whacked. Eight times round the rugby pitch and that was before we played a game!'

'You're doing tea,' Mum pointed at Grump. 'No arguing.'

'Aw, Mum, it's not my turn.' Grump's face lived up to his nick-name.

'Just do it. You lads take your turn, like the rest of us,' replied Mum.

'Dad never does it,' piped up Sal. 'Anyway, when will he be home?'

'He's got a sleep-over, tonight. Devon somewhere. Then Carlisle, day after tomorrow.'

Dad was a long-distance lorry driver. Sal thought it must be nice to escape from all this noise into a lorry and drive all day. You would never have to help make the tea, or change nappies or trip over loads of kids in the house. If any of them had been in her room today she would half kill them.

'What happened to the tea, then?' Mum asked as the boys joined her at the table, their slices of bread slowly

11

oozing dark chocolate spread.

'Here it is. Sugar in the bowl.' Sal grinned and shoved the tray onto the table before running upstairs. She jumped on her bed. Laughter took hold of her and her whole body shook. Any minute now she would hear the explosion.

'You little. . . .' that was Boss. Sounded like he had tipped his chair over.

'I'll murder you,' Grump joined in. 'You're such a pain.' He was charging up the stairs. Mum was in hot pursuit.

'Sally! Sal-lee! Come here at once. You wait 'til I get you.' Sal dived off her bed as the door burst open. 'You little toad!'

'Toad!' screeched Boss. 'Can't you call her anything else?'

'Course I can,' replied Mum, 'but not in front of you lot.' Turning to Sal, she drew a deep breath and began. 'Get down into that kitchen at once. Clear up all the mess. Wash up. Mop the floor and make yourself scarce. If you ever do that again you'll wish you'd never been born!'

Sal took one look at Mum's face and ran downstairs. The 'littlies', as she called the children that Mum minded, were all crowding into the kitchen. Paul had wanted to see what all the fuss was about and had taken a big gulp from one of the mugs of tea. The fact that it was heavily loaded with salt, not sugar, had made him sick. Right on the dirty rugby kit.

Sal burst out laughing. Her tricks got better. Two in one day! Well the gang might not like them at school, but this one at home had been ace. Even worth cleaning the kitchen up for. The look on Grump's face! He always was a greedy pig. He must have had an enormous swig of tea and now he looked like a greenish prune. What a joke!

She could hear Mum trying to calm her brothers down and it sounded as if the TV was blasting out louder than ever. Sal finished her tasks, picked up the rugby kit and threw it into the washer and added her own school skirt. Rescuing her treasures from the pockets, a broken ruler, ball of wool, penknife with no blade, half-chewed gum and two rubber bands, she stuffed the skirt at the back. That way mum would not see today's mud and tomato sauce stains.

Still in her jumper and knickers, Sal went upstairs to her room. She had had her laugh; now down to business. The project. Mum had ignored her and something told Sal that it was no use asking her to help. Dad was always working. Boss and Grump were a dead loss. All Grump did was play sport and listen to music. Dad had told him for years that he was built like a rugby player and Grump had obviously listened to him. He was huge, yet could run around the pitch really fast. Sal knew. She had seen him. Once. She had moaned so much about standing around in the cold, that Dad had never taken her again to watch.

Boss might have helped her. He would have before Julie. Julie was his girlfriend. Boss spent hours in the bathroom, smelt awful, and kept asking Mum for money to go places. He had grown a lot taller but was still as thin as a rake. He had made his dark hair go straight back from his forehead, so that he looked like a pop singer. Sal had seen him go out one night in Dad's leather jacket, the one Mum had bought him for Christmas out of the catalogue. Boss had to pay Sal a large bar of chocolate every Saturday so she would not tell that she had seen him. What he saw in Julie was beyond her. She looked so much like a *girl*. All long legs and dresses and earrings and stuff. I'll never go like that, she thought, as she slipped into her oldest jeans, the ones with the double hole in the knee.

Sal lay on her bed, gazing around for ideas. The room wasn't very inspiring. Her bed was squashed up under the window from which there was the exciting view of the back yard and the house behind them. Sal used to spy on their neighbours, inventing stories about them, although Mr and Mrs Exhall, in their late sixties, lived the most ordinary lives you could imagine. In fact the most interesting thing that had ever happened to them was in last year's storm. A chimney pot had crashed through the roof of the outside toilet. The way Mr Exhall had gone on, you'd have thought the whole house was about to collapse.

She looked round the rest of the room. One tatty wardrobe, door open and bulging with clothes, one old, dark chest of drawers that looked as if it had come out of the ark, and about two square metres of floor space. The old striped carpet was completely covered with the strewn contents of her school bag, her pyjamas and kicked off shoes. Hardly the place to think up projects.

Still, back to Easter . . . hmm, let's think. Eggs and chicks, sometimes new clothes; visit to Grandma's – that's no good. And, of course, a story. She heard it every year. This man, Jesus, had died on a wooden cross. Actually he wasn't really a man, he was God. If he was God, how could he have died? And anyway didn't he come alive again? Although how anyone could do that was beyond her. She would steer away from the Jesus bit about Easter. Yes, I'll stick to chicks and eggs and things, she thought. Eggs should be easy. A lot easier than dying and being God and coming alive again. That was far too complicated.

3

'Sal, you got any ideas for the project?' asked Narrinder, twirling her long plaits round like skipping ropes.

Sal looked into her friend's deep brown eyes. What could she reply? If she told Narrinder of her idea, then they would have to share the prize. Why couldn't Narrinder think of something for herself?

'Don't know,' she answered eventually. 'I think we're supposed to do the project on our own.'

'Miss Winter said we can do it in groups. Go on, Sal, please. You know we always work together.'

'Only if I get to keep the prize,' Sal said finally. 'And you don't tell anyone what we're going to do. Not even Tag and Cowboy.'

'Course,' Narrinder was relieved. Sal always had the best ideas.

'We'll do nests.'

'Nests?'

'Yes, lots of them. Everyone will do chickens. We'll do a nest each for a hen, a duck, a blackbird, goose. . . . and what else?'

'How about a turkey nest,' Narrinder was getting the idea. 'Or a swan's, or . . . or a tortoise.'

'Tortoise! Don't be so daft,' Sal thought her friend had gone stupid.

'Yes. Tortoise. They lay eggs. I know. I've seen one.' Narrinder defended her idea.

'I know, we'll just do nests for things we can actually get the eggs for. Then we can put an egg in each one, with a label saying what it is.' Sal's mind was working fast. In fact Narrinder would come in useful. Her dad owned the corner shop by the school. He sold everything. Narrinder could get him to buy some weird eggs for the project.

Her thoughts were interrupted by Narrinder. 'But, Sal. Listen. It's got to go on the wall. We can't put real eggs on the wall!'

''Course we can. Superglue. Tonight get your dad to give you some. And you've got to find lots of different eggs. I'll get an ordinary hen's one out of our fridge. And I'll do the thinking. Understand?'

Narrinder understood. Trust her to get the hard part. She'd never even seen a turkey or goose egg and now she had to find them. Still it was better than trying to do the project on her own.

By Saturday morning the girls were ready to put their project together. They met in Narrinder's huge attic bedroom in the flat above the shop.

Sal loved it there, it was so spacious. Strange and wonderful smells drifted up from the shop downstairs. Everything matched. All the furniture was white with red handles. None of the handles was broken. The thick red carpet covered the vast floor and the white wallpaper with tiny red flowers on it, was just the same as the curtains and duvet cover. Narrinder even had her own television and stereo system. When Sal had moaned about her own poky room and requested a TV, Mum had muttered things about, 'It's all right for some people,' and that had been the end of that.

It was a great place to do a project.

Sal had persuaded Miss Winter to give them an enormous piece of card. Every night they had collected twigs, moss, bits of straw and dead leaves. It had not been easy. Most of the houses round them did not have front gardens and the back yards were mostly full of bikes, junk and wet washing. So the girls had visited the park to scavenge what they could. Now they had two carrier bags full of bits and pieces, ready for the nests.

The hen's was easy. A clump of straw with a hollow in it. It was a good job that they had helped themselves to a bundle of the school rabbit's bedding! They had to guess for the goose nest but decided to do a bigger mound of straw with no hollow in it.

'Now the duck's,' said Sal, sitting back on her heels. 'We'll use some sticks and feathers.'

'Feathers?'

'Well, yes, makes it look different. And we've got some.' The sticks were super-glued into place.

'It'll never stay on the card,' commented Narrinder.

'Stop moaning. Course it will. We'll put more glue on it every day after school. Now you come up with an idea for the turkey.'

'I've never seen a turkey nest,' Narrinder thought out loud. 'Don't they live in batteries, like hens?

'We could get some old batteries, get the middles out and stick eggs inside them,' said Sal.

'Trouble is, they're too small. We need something big.'

'Like Dad's lorry battery. It's enormous. Mum went mad when he fiddled with it on the kitchen table. Got acid or something on the wood.' Sal giggled at the memory. 'It'd look dead good next to this lot.'

Narrinder started to laugh as well. 'At least,' she began, trying to catch her breath, 'Miss Winter would have to give us marks for . . . what did she call it?'

'Being creative,' Sal said. 'Well it'd certainly be different. Go on, let's do it.'

'Would your dad give it you?'

Sal paused. Would he? 'Not likely!' she said, 'But it's

still a good idea. Perhaps we'd better think of something else.'

In the end they drew a grid shape and attached some bits of wire from two coat hangers to it.

'There,' said Sal satisfied. 'Looks like a cage. Now for the eggs.'

Narrinder's dad had come up trumps. Well he had had to. His daughter had behaved as if the world would end if he did not supply the right eggs.

'We've got to blow them. Get the insides out, Dad said so,' Narrinder tried to insist but Sal took no notice.

'No time. Anyway, *I'm* not blowing them. You can.'

'Can't. Makes me feel sick even to think of it.'

'Well stop going on and help me to stick them into place.'

The project looked very impressive. At least it did on the floor. Four nests and four real eggs with Easter written in green and yellow felt pen in the middle. Getting it upright and to school might prove difficult, but Sal's faith in superglue was unshakeable. It would be fine. The best project ever. But still two weeks until they could hand it in. They would never wait that long!

However there was one exciting day left before the end of term. 1st April. April Fools' Day.

The gang agreed that it was okay to trick people that day, even at school. Every break time secret meetings took place while they tried to think of what to do. It had got to be good, and funny.

Vicki and her friend Brian the Brain were always hanging around them.

'Why don't you two push off!' said Sal angrily one lunch time.

'We want to join your gang. Brian has great ideas and my mummy will let you all meet at our house,' Vicki's posh whining voice really irritated Sal. She would have to put her foot down or the others would let them join the gang. They all wanted to see what lay behind the sparkling white net curtains of Vicki's big house on the edge of the estate. They had all been curious about her ever since last term when she had turned up, the only new girl in the class. Sal was not going to let her into the gang. She might take over and then Sal would never get them all to agree with her ideas.

Pushing her fringe out of her eyes, she stood up as tall as she could, which was not very tall, and looked Vicki straight in the eyes.

'I've said, push off. That means go, get lost, vanish. We don't want you creeping around us.' Vicki got the message and drifted off across the playground looking sad and dejected in her smart new coat and sheepskin gloves. Brian trailed after her, kicking a paper bag with his big feet. He turned and glared at Sal, but didn't look very frightening, with his big blue eyes and brown hair that stuck up like a loo brush.

'Aw, Sal, she's all right,' began Tag, gesturing with his arms that hung like sausages from his shrunken anorak sleeves.

'Shut up. Now come on. Ideas for April Fools' Day.' Being leader of this gang was hard work. Tag and even Cowboy were starting to boss *her* around. That would never do!

Early on 1st April Sal woke to the sound of a roar, like a mad lion. It seemed Dad had found the margarine smeared all over the bathroom door handle. She waited for the next outburst. She didn't have to wait long.

'That daughter of yours . . .' stormed Dad to Mum. 'She's worse than the boys ever were. I'm covered in it.'

'It' was what you get when you take most of the toothpaste out of a tube and refill it with water. Probably squirts quite a long way, especially when squeezed by an angry, sleepy Dad. Probably gone all over his prickly brown beard. Sal wished that she could see him. He must look so funny. Better stay in bed, though, and pretend she was asleep. Pity she had not thought of any more tricks to do at home. Still this morning at school should make up for that.

Lessons really dragged until at last it was time for Art. There had been a few feeble attempts by the rest of the class to trick people, like putting the wrong date on the blackboard, pretending Brian was off ill when he was only in the loo, and sticking chewing-gum on teacher's chair. But they were all pathetic compared with what was to come.

The class drifted in and out of the room, fetching water, cleaning paintbrushes, milling around, supposedly painting pictures of spring.

'Now,' whispered Sal. She slipped out of the room, down the corridor and to the cupboard outside the secretary's office. Swiftly opening the door, she pulled down the metal handle marked 'Fire Alarm Practice Bell.' What a din! On and on the buzzer went. Racing back to the classroom, she lined up with the others. Good, no sign of the rest of the gang.

All the classes streamed out into the playground. Tag, Cowboy and Narrinder quickly joined 3N. They had done their bit. All the blackboards had April Fools! written on them in big chalk letters. Well, not quite all. Tag's brain had gone into overload with all the excitement and he had written 'April Fuels!' but the message was still clear enough.

It certainly was to Miss Winter when they all trooped back into the classroom. The cold wind outside had made her usually pale cheeks bright red. They clashed with her orangey lipstick and brown eye make-up, which normally looked just right with her mousy hair with blonde highlights.

Now she stood stamping her feet in her brown boots and rubbing her hands together in front of the class.

'Very funny,' she said. 'Absolutely hilarious, I'm sure. I don't expect anyone here knows why the alarm went off, do they?' She gazed around the room, fairly certain who was responsible. No reply. Ah, well, they could have thought up something worse.

Sal was so proud of herself. The whole school and teachers, even the Head, and the kitchen staff. All of them outside because of her . . . and the gang, of course. What a superb trick! No one would ever guess who it was. April Fools' day was a smashing idea.

4

That afternoon, when the twelve o'clock deadline for playing tricks was past, some normality returned to class 3N. There were two and a half days left until the end of term and Miss Winter was trying to encourage everybody to finish their projects.

'I'm sure many of you have been working very hard,' she said. 'Now don't forget, you are to bring them on Thursday and I'll tell you on Friday who has won the prizes. Now, any questions about the project?'

'Please, Miss.' It was Narrinder. Surely she wasn't going to let on what her and Sal's project was. 'Can my dad help us bring our project to school? It's a bit big and me and Sal might break it.'

'Of course,' smiled Miss Winter. 'I can't wait to see what you two have come up with. Tell your dad that I'll be here a bit earlier on Thursday. Now any more questions? . . . No . . . Well, this afternoon I want us to carry on with the Easter story. Who can remember where we are up to?'

As usual Brian's hand shot up. He was amazing really. You'd never guess he was clever. He sat by the window and spent most of the time looking out of it. Anyone else would get told off for daydreaming. But not Brian. Oh, no. As soon as Miss asked a question he was right on the ball, nearly always with the correct answer.

Miss Winter waited until a few more arms joined

Brian's, waving around like an assortment of brightly coloured wrinkled elephants' trunks.

'Yes, Vicki,' she said.

'Well, Miss,' Vicki took a deep breath.' Jesus had been on this donkey ride and everyone liked him and cheered him. Then a few days later they didn't like him any more. He went to this garden – Gathme . . .'

'Gethsemane,' interrupted Brian.

'Anyway,' Vicki wasn't put off from telling her story, 'anyway it was dark. Some soldiers came. His friend . . .'

'Judas!' shouted Brian.

'His friend kissed him and then the soldiers knew which one was Jesus. So they took him away somewhere.' Vicki paused triumphantly and waited for Miss Winter to say something encouraging to her.

'That's right, Vicki. Well done. Now we come to the next part of the story. The part we celebrate and remember on Good Friday. Who knows what happened next? Yes, Tom?'

'They put Jesus on a cross and he died.'

'That's right. Does anyone know what happened before that?'

Apparently not. Even Brian seemed stumped.

'I'll read you part of the story from the Bible so we can see what happened.'

Miss Winter started to read. It was quite a long story. Jesus was arrested, beaten, given a sort of trial by some rulers called Pilate and Herod and then sentenced to death. He was nailed to a cross and after a few hours he died. There were a lot of people watching and after he had died, they took him away to be buried. It was a horrible way to die, and, as Jesus had done nothing wrong, it was completely unfair. Quite unjust, as Miss Winter was saying.

As Sal listened to the story, she began to think. Why?

Why did they hate Jesus so much that they had to kill him? Why didn't he stop them? If he was God he could have . . . well . . . he could have stuck up for himself, struck them all dead. Or done an amazing trick so they would have *had* to believe that he was God. He didn't fight back. That just didn't make sense. If she'd been there, she would have stopped them killing him. She'd have stuck up for him all right.

Miss Winter finished.

'Now,' she said, 'for the rest of the afternoon, which isn't much, we're going across to St Peter's church. Mr Rogers, the curate, is going to show us something and then tomorrow we'll all have lots of ideas for our Easter work.'

Sal was glad to get out. She didn't like the story about Jesus. Well, not today's part. The other stories about when he was born, or healed people of awful illnesses, or gave them loads of bread and fish; – well, those stories were good. They were interesting, but this one today, okay, she'd heard it all before, but today she'd really listened. And she didn't like it at all. I wish it hadn't happened, she thought. It's so unfair. Jesus was good. Why on earth did he have to die, and like that too?

Eventually 3N lined up at the school gate, chattering and playing. Like a wriggly worm they walked down the street until they came to St Peter's church. It was huge, ancient, its big stones covered in black grime. Sal had never been in it although she knew there was a modern hall round the back somewhere, where Boss and Grump went to the Youth Group. Mum always said she pitied anyone who got married there. The photos would be awful, what with the sooty old walls on one side and the thundering traffic on the other.

Inside the church was better. It took your eyes a few minutes to adjust to the dim light. The walls were white, at least where the plaster had not peeled off. Miss Winter marched them to the front and told them all to look sideways.

The struggling mid-afternoon sun filtered through a huge stained-glass window, bathing the cold concrete floor of the church with a kaleidoscope of warm colours.

'It's beautiful, Miss,' said Narrinder.

'Yes,' replied Miss Winter. She raised her voice so they could all hear. 'Mr Rogers has very kindly opened the church for us today, so that we could look at this beautiful window. Perhaps you'd just explain it to us, Mr Rogers.'

Mr Rogers smiled. He didn't look like a curate, well not like the ones on the telly. He was quite young, with lots of wild curly hair and he was wearing jeans and the sort of denim jacket that Sal's brother, Grump, had been wanting for ages.

He started to tell them how stained-glass windows were made, how this one had survived the bombing in the war and how it told a story.

'If you start at the top left-hand corner . . . you'll see the birth of Jesus. Now move across a bit . . . there, what's that?'

'Jesus and his friends,' mumbled the class.

'Disciples,' Brian couldn't resist giving them their proper name.

'That's right – then we see the feeding of the five thousand, the healing of the leper . . .'

'Looks like my mum in her nightie,' whispered Tag to Sal, who, seeing the resemblance, started to giggle quietly, until Miss Winter gave her 'The Look' which shut her up. She started to listen again.

'. . . and here is where Jesus rose from the dead, and lastly when he went back to heaven. We call that the Ascension.' Mr Rogers finally finished and after the children had had a good wander around the building, Miss Winter lined them up for the walk back to school.

'Right,' she began, huddling herself deep into her fluffy lined anorak, which Tag said his sister thought was from Marks and Spencer, 'tomorrow we're going to make our own stained-glass window, in class. We've had some lovely ideas from David . . . I mean Mr Rogers,' she beamed at him and Mr Rogers went red, 'and we can do the Easter story on our windows.'

'Sounds fun,' said Narrinder.

'Hey Nar,' asked Tag. 'Don't your mum and dad mind you coming to that church and doing about Jesus and stuff?'

'No, it's okay,' Narrinder smiled. 'We have our own gods at home and I go to the temple. Mum says it's good for me to see what others think. Anyway, that way I get Easter eggs as well as special sweets at our celebrations.'

Best of both worlds, thought Sal. Mind you, Narrinder's mum always gave her as many Indian sweets as she could eat. The orange marzipan ones were the nicest. In fact if they went back to Narrinder's, she was sure they'd have some and they could just put a bit more glue on the project.

So half an hour later the two girls, sticky with glue and marzipan sweets, surveyed their work. It looked great. Narrinder had pushed her bed under the window to make more room, and the project lay in the middle of the floor in all its glory.

'It's a bit big,' said Narrinder. 'We'll never get it upright.'

'Come on. We'll have a practice run. You hold this corner . . . and this bit. I'll grab this end. Now lift . . .'

And lift they did.

'Gosh, it's heavy. Look Sal, it's sagging in the middle, by the goose nest. It'll rip.'

'It's okay. Look, let's put it down. It'll be fine pinned onto the wall. Let's just glue these chunks of straw a bit more.'

At last they were totally satisfied with their work. Narrinder's dad popped up from the shop.

'Marvellous,' he said, gazing round the room which now resembled a stable. 'Be here at half past eight, Sal, and we'll put it in the van. And after school you can help Narrinder clean up this mess.' He paused as he started downstairs. 'And the next time you have a project, you can do it at Sal's house!'

'Okay,' yelled the two girls in unison, at his departing back, 'We will.'

If only tomorrow would hurry up and come. The prize was as good as theirs!

5

By eight o'clock Sal was at Narrinder's. As usual the shop was open. Sal's mum said it was never shut and Sal half believed her.

Barging her way past the aisles of foodstuffs, Sal went through the door into the living area.

'Narrinder!' she yelled. 'Where's your dad?' Sal had looked around. There was no sign of him although Narrinder's older brother and a couple of uncles were already busy in the shop.

'She's upstairs,' Narrinder's mum turned towards her, pausing in her task of making chappaties on the stove. 'Her dad's at the cash-and-carry. He'll be back.'

Sal shot upstairs. Narrinder wasn't even dressed! This house was as mad as her own, first thing in the morning.

'Come on, we've got to get to school.'

Narrinder smiled. For once Sal would have to wait for her, instead of always taking the lead.

'We've plenty of time,' she said, stretching gracefully as she got into her jumper. 'Dad'll be back. He said we weren't to move it until he got home.'

The minutes ticked by so slowly that Sal could have screamed. Then they heard the van pull up and Narrinder's dad and brother, Suliman, came into the room.

'Grief, it pongs in here,' said Suliman. 'What have you been doing?'

'This,' said Sal, pointing to the project. Suliman, for

once, was lost for words.

At last the project was flat in the back of the van, and driving very slowly, they reached school. The blue van halted, and as the back door opened, first Sal, then Suliman, then Dad and Narrinder emerged backwards, crouched over something the size of a dining table. Together they got it into the classroom and, after much grunting and shifting bodies out of the way, the project was drawing-pinned, blu-tacked and stapled to the wall.

All stepped back to admire it. A few stray strands of straw fluttered lazily onto the floor.

'It's . . . it's . . .' Miss Winter seemed to be stuck for what to say.

'It's very creative, Miss,' piped up Sal.

'Created a right mess, I can tell you.' That was Narrinder's dad.

'Yes. Creative. Very . . . and original . . . and well stuck together.' Miss Winter turned and thanked them for their efforts, as the rest of class 3N started to trickle in.

Everyone agreed that Sal's and Narrinder's project was certainly the biggest and the messiest! But was it the best? Miss Winter wasn't saying.

'The winners will be announced tomorrow,' she declared, after assembly. 'Now today we're going to work on our stained-glass windows. In groups. I want you to work out a design on a piece of paper. Remember, it's some part of the Easter story. Keep it simple as we'll make the windows out of coloured tissue paper and black tape.'

General commotion broke out. Miss Winter restored order. Sitting on her desk, she clapped her hands together. 'Before we begin, we need to finish off the story. We'll read round, from the Bible, what happened next. Starting with you Brian, one verse each.'

They zoomed through this bit. It was much more

simple. Jesus came alive again, did things with his friends and went back to heaven.

Simple, it might be, thought Sal, but she was finding the whole thing really confusing. Why die and then come alive again? Wouldn't it have been much easier just to have stayed alive all the time?

Her thoughts were interrupted by Miss Winter.

'Now then, you four,' she said looking at Sal, Narrinder, Tag and Cowboy, 'Which bit do you want to work on?'

'The donkey ride,' said Cowboy.

'Sorry, Vicki's table is doing that.'

'Well, the soldiers and crosses and things,' Cowboy tried again.

'No,' interrupted Sal.

'No?' queried Miss Winter.

'I don't like that bit. Can't we do when he comes alive again?'

In the end they compromised. Cowboy and Tag worked on colourful soldiers, while Sal and Narrinder cut out tissue paper trees and grass for the garden where Jesus had risen from the dead.

By the afternoon they were ready to start sticking. In their groups, the children balanced on chairs and tried to get everything on the window. Cowboy had produced so many soldiers that he was taping them up everywhere.

'You can't put one on the donkey, with Jesus,' whispered Sal. 'Looks stupid.' She was getting cross. Tissue paper tears very easily and her trees looked like half chewed slices of cucumber by now. The black tape was great for sticking, especially your fingers to one another. Miss Winter patiently helped them and the picture slowly started to come alive.

'Look, Miss,' said Tag, 'the sun's coming out. Like in church.'

Everyone stopped to look as blue, green and yellow

shapes danced across the classroom walls.

As they looked, there was a strange sound. A sort of sludge – slurp – plop. Quite gentle and quiet. In fact no one really noticed it.

A terrible smell filled the room. Like stink bombs, stale food, Grump's rugby boots all rolled into one. Vicki began to cough and heave and dashed out of the room only to be sick before reaching the toilets.

'Miss, what is it?'

'Cor, it's awful.'

'Can we go out?'

'Vicki's been sick.'

Miss Winter told all the children to go to the cloak-room while she investigated. It didn't take long. She soon found the cause of the awful pong. Super-glue was not as super as Sal had believed. One of the eggs had slowly come unstuck, rolled off its nest and crashed onto the floor. As she watched, a second egg joined it, spilling its foul, rotten contents onto the floor and splashing them up the wall.

Shooting into the corridor, Miss Winter, grabbed Sal.

'You stupid girl,' she yelled. 'You used real eggs. Real ones!'

'Yes, of course,' Sal wondered what all the fuss was about.

'You didn't blow them – clean them out.'

Sal was silent. Hadn't Narrinder told her that her dad said they must blow them?

'They're rotten. Awful. Smashed. Now you and Nar-rinder can clean the lot up and put it in the big bins.' She paused and turned to the rest of the class. 'Right, the rest of us will have to use the library. Move.'

'But Miss,' Sal queried. 'Haven't we won the competition?'

'Won it! *Won it*! You must be joking. Just take the whole revolting mess out of my classroom. Now!' Miss

Winter just managed to control her temper.

Sal looked at Narrinder. What were they to do? All their hopes and plans had gone wrong. Okay, so the eggs bit hadn't worked. But the rest of the project! The nests. They were great. It wasn't fair that they had to go as well.

'It's not fair,' muttered Sal to Narrinder. 'Why can't we just clean the eggs up?'

'We'd better do what she says. Don't tell my dad, will you? He'll have a fit, what with letting us do it at my house, and bringing it here.'

'Course I won't say. I thought we'd won. It's much better than this lot.' Sal pointed fiercely at the other competition entries. She felt like crying. All their hard work for nothing. Well, for worse than nothing. For getting told off, and having to destroy their project. Miss Winter had done it on purpose. She had never wanted Sal to win. That was it. Well she'd think of a way to get even with her.

6

Sal was still in a bad mood when she got home.

Slamming the door behind her, she stormed into the living room, removed one of the 'littlies' from an armchair and stared at the flickering television screen. The 'littly', in this case a dungareed three-year-old, was not happy at this treatment and started to bawl his head off.

Mum swooped over and picked him up, like the hawk catching a mouse Sal had seen on a TV wildlife programme.

'Whatever's up with you? You go out at the crack of dawn, singing your head off, and come home as if the world's ended,' demanded Mum.

'It has,' Sal replied glumly. 'It's all her fault.'

She told Mum what had happened. Mum must be going funny in the head because instead of telling her off, she started to laugh and laugh. The 'littlies' joined in, not knowing what was going on.

'Oh, Sal,' gasped Mum, wiping her streaming eyes, her chest still heaving, sending the two pandas on today's jumper jigging around, 'you are a case. Wait till I tell your dad. I'd have loved to have been there.'

'Well, it was awful. I'm going upstairs.' No one understood her. By the time Mum had told Dad, her brothers, the mums who would fetch the 'littlies' and half the street, Sal would be the laughing stock of the town. Well, let them laugh. She'd show them that two could play that game. She'd come up with a trick or two yet. Then she could laugh at them.

She lay on her bed for ages, listening to them all downstairs. Eventually there was a knock on her door and Grump came in with a stupid grin on his silly fat face.

'Mum says you're to come down for tea. We're having poached eggs! Just for you.'

Sal picked up a stuffed toy whale and threw it at him, but he was too quick. She'd get him later. As for now, she would act all grown-up and be calm and keep above all the teasing.

'Ah, the eggs-pert project maker,' said Boss, 'Come to grace us with her presence.'

Sal glowered at him but kept quiet. 'Heard you've had an eggs-xiting day,' said Dad, who was washing his hands in the sink. 'Eggstraordinary'.

'Must have scrambled your brains to come up with an idea like that.' That was Grump's contribution.

'Don't worry Sal, it's only a yolk.'

Once Boss and Grump got their double act working there was no stopping them. Sal ignored them and eventually the conversation topic changed.

'Mum, is my red shirt ready for tonight?' asked Boss. 'I've got to have it.'

'Where are you going then?' asked Dad. He was on his second mug of tea and working out how many matches his football team needed to win to stay in the Second Division. The back of the folded newspaper was covered in little sums. Every two minutes Grump told him he'd got a sum wrong and that the team was rubbish anyway.

'It's the Youth Club Easter disco, tonight,' said Boss. 'Me and him,' pointing to his brother, 'are in charge of the music. David said we could do it and bring our own tapes and things. We've got a couple of party tapes and three "Hits Now" cassettes. That should keep us going.'

'Can I come?'

'Course not . . . It's for teenagers, not daft little kids like you.'

Right, thought Sal, I'll show you who's a daft little kid then, big brother. I can think of a way you won't look so great at the disco tonight. In fact I bet Julie will think you're a right wally, red shirt or not.

She went to the front of the house. Oh good. Dad's lorry was there. Well it wasn't actually his lorry but he always drove it. Sometimes if he had to leave very early the next day, he would bring it home. Old Mrs Evans, next door, used to moan and say it blocked her light but she never complained directly to Dad. There were some advantages in being very tall and built like a wrestler.

Finding Dad's jacket, she retrieved the lorry's key and crept out of the front door. Balancing on the wheel arch, she unlocked the cab and searched around. Ah, there they were. Dad wouldn't notice they were missing tonight. Such funny names – Stravinsky, Debussy and Brahms. No wonder that the others were always teasing Dad about his taste in music. He didn't mind. He said that it helped him relax, especially in traffic jams.

After replacing the keys, Sal scuttled up to her brothers' room. Good, no sign of them. Grump was helping in the kitchen and Boss would be hours in the bath, as usual. Quickly she did what she had to do, and checking that everything was as she had found it, went back downstairs.

A little later on Sal thought, now for Mum. Sal was bathing Lizzie who squealed with delight, as she trickled the bubbly water over her.

Sal wrapped Lizzie in a big towel and, perched on the edge of the bath, began to dry her, tickling her as she went.

'Well, little Lizzie,' she said, 'Your bubbles have given me an idea. Good job you can't talk much yet and give me away. Come on, down to the kitchen.'

Lizzie chuckled and bumped her way down the stairs on her bottom.

'What are you doing?' shouted Mum, from the living room.

'Just getting Lizzie her bedtime bottle,' yelled Sal. 'Be back in a minute.'

Quickly she went over to the washing machine, opened the little drawer and poured the rest of Lizzie's bubble bath into it. Mum always put the washer on overnight so she could hang out the wet clothes in the morning. Tomorrow she would be in for a surprise!

Later that evening Sal was woken by angry voices from downstairs. Quietly stealing out of bed, she inched her way to the door so that she could hear better.

'I looked a complete fool.' That was Boss. 'A real idiot. You should have heard what Julie said.'

'And David,' added Grump. 'Loads of stuff about trusting us, and doing a good job, and all that.'

'Well, what happened?' asked Mum, bewildered.

'Debussy, that's what, Debussy or Brahms.'

'Debussy or Brahms? What on earth are you talking about?'

'It's her. That Sal. It must be,' said Grump. 'It couldn't be anyone else. No one else would do it.'

'Do what?' Mum was getting annoyed.

'Swapped all our tapes. No "Hits Now" cassettes, just Dad's classical stuff. I put the first tape on, to warm us up, and out came this soppy, romantic orchestra. I nearly died,' said Boss.

'All the rest were the same, or worse,' added Grump. 'We couldn't do anything about it. It was too far to come back from Micklesford to get the proper tapes.'

'Well, what did you do?' that was Dad, sounding sleepy. He must have been in bed when the boys returned.

'Do? Well nothing really. Mr Rogers had a "Hits of the Sixties" tape in the minibus. We had to dance to that. It was pathetic. I'm going to kill Sal.' Boss sounded as though he meant it.

'Leave it to me,' said Dad. 'I'll see to her, when I get back tomorrow night. She's got to realise that her stupid tricks cause trouble, Now, let's all get to bed. I've got to leave at six in the morning.'

Sal snuggled back into bed. Daft little kid, eh? She had shown them. Mind you, Dad was mad at her. Perhaps it would have been better not to have done the washing machine trick. It was too late now. She could hear the quiet rumble of the machine. Mum must just have turned it on. Oh, well, it might not be too bad.

But it *was* bad. As the family lay sleeping, bubbles oozed their way out of the washing machine and stealthily crawled across the kitchen floor, stopping only briefly to make sticky piles against the bottom of the chairs and cupboard doors.

Sal didn't hear Dad leave at six but she certainly heard Mum get up. A dressing-gowned figure shook her awake.

'Get up,' hissed Mum. 'You, young lady, have gone too far, this time, much too far.' She dragged Sal downstairs. The bubbles had popped by now, but everything was covered in a pink sticky mess.

'I know that it's you,' said Mum. 'You ruined your brothers' evening, and ruined my washing. It's going to take hours to clean up this mess. You've upset me, your dad, everyone. What have you got to say?'

'I didn't mean to. It was only a trick. A joke.'

'A joke!!' screeched Mum. 'If you ever try out another joke here, you'll wish you'd never been born. Dad was going to deal with you tonight, for what you did to the boys, but I can't wait that long.'

Mum was furious. She grabbed Sal roughly by her pyjama top and forced her to sit down.

'Right, you'll be punished for this, and punished hard. No television until after the Easter holidays, and no pocket money either. Understand?'

'Yes, Mum, I'm sorry.'

'Sorry! You will be. Now, get a bowl of cereal and go to your room until school time. If your brothers even see you, I won't be responsible for what happens!'

Slowly Sal went back to her room. Why hadn't everyone laughed at her tricks? Perhaps it was true. Perhaps those sort of tricks just hurt people and weren't really funny. The whole family were mad at her and she didn't like that. There was only one thing she could do. She would just have to change. The tricks would have to stop, however hard she found it. That was it. She would make a New Year's resolution. Only it wasn't New Year. Never mind. My Easter resolution she thought. No more tricks.

7

By the end of the day, Sal had come to the conclusion that keeping resolutions was hard. In fact it was nearly impossible. There were so many opportunities to tease someone, or hide their crayons, or to pretend something had happened when it hadn't.

All in all, the last day of term was a flop. At least the revolting stink had gone out of the classroom. So had the beautiful project. There was a big gap on the back wall where it had been. All round the gap the other projects were displayed. They were really boringly uninteresting. Sal's and Narrinder's work would have won the prize easily, if the stupid eggs had stayed on.

'Well, children,' Miss Winter was trying to get their attention. 'After the excitement of yesterday, we all need to work hard to get our stained-glass window finished. It's coming on really well. In fact Mr Rogers is coming in this afternoon to have a look at it, and to give out the project prizes.'

'Do you fancy him, Miss?' That was Cowboy, squirming around on his seat and grinning at the rest of the class.

Miss Winter ignored him, but she looked a bit pink in the face as she walked over to the back wall. Sal noticed that she was wearing a new jumper and skirt in shades of brown. It was quite trendy. What a laugh if Miss liked Mr Rogers! She caught Cowboy's eye and winked. It would be worth investigating what was going on.

Pointing to the projects, Miss Winter was telling everyone how wonderful they were. 'And of course I think we all have to admit that Sal's and Narrinder's was the most creative . . .'

They were going to get the prize after all, Sal thought, unable to stop herself breaking into a huge smile.

'However,' continued Miss Winter, 'they were careless and didn't think enough about what they were doing, and we all know the results of that!'

Didn't think! Didn't think enough! Sal was furious. Her face turned an angry red as she clenched her hands round her straggly hair which was escaping from its bunches. They'd thought and thought. It wasn't their fault that super-glue was useless. Everyone knew that the prize was theirs by right.

'So I have chosen this one for the first prize.'

'This one' was a sickly yellow cardboard chicken which popped out of a neatly coloured nest, complete with foil paper eggs.

'A round of applause then for Vicki,' Miss Winter continued. 'You've done very well. Congratulations.'

Vicki! 'Bet her mum made it,' hissed Sal to Narrinder. 'She's never done that on her own. Look at her.'

Vicki looked so pleased with herself, plonked there at her desk, podgy hands clasped neatly in front of her. It wasn't fair that she, of all people, should win.

For the rest of the morning Sal worked half-heartedly at her bit of the window. Every time she caught sight of Vicki she felt sick. And she caught sight of her rather a lot, as Vicki was working on the next section to her.

'Shame about your project,' whispered Vicki, 'I thought it was really good.' She wanted, so much, to be friends with Sal and her gang. 'Tell you what, we can share the prize, after school, by the gates. Shall we?' She smiled up at Sal, unable to understand why Sal had excluded her in the past.

Sal didn't understand why she hated her either. Somehow she felt threatened by Vicki. If she was in the gang, the rest of them might like Vicki more than her. She just couldn't risk it, although the thought of chocolate was tempting.

Turning slowly, Sal pretended to stick a piece of tissue paper on the window, right by Vicki's face.

Deliberately she began, 'I wouldn't share your chocolate if you were the only person left on earth. If I was starving. You can stuff your chocolate where you like, but keep away from me.'

Vicki's round face crumpled, rather like the tissue paper, and she quickly looked the other way, determined that Sal would not see that she was trying not to cry. Right, that settled it. Never again would she try to be friends with Sal. She'd think of a way of getting her own back on her. Brian would help her. She'd show Sal what it felt like to be treated like dirt. In fact, if she could think up a good enough plan, the gang would end up her friends, not Sal's. She had all the Easter holidays to work out how to teach Sal a lesson.

The Easter holidays were a bore. Sal's mum was even busier than usual with the 'littlies' and had Paul, the six-year-old cassette recorder wrecker all day. Mum stuck to her word and would not let Sal watch TV or give her any pocket money. There's not a lot you can do when you've no money and it rains nearly all the time.

Only one thing livened up the holidays. The gang had decided to trail Miss Winters and Mr Rogers. This was a bit difficult because no one knew where Miss Winter lived and Mr Rogers always seemed to be at the church.

'It's 'cos it's Easter,' said Tag. 'Bet he has to do overtime.'

The breakthrough came one Friday.

'Saw your teacher, yesterday,' volunteered Grump. 'Angela, isn't it?'

'Angela?' So that's what the A stood for in A. Winter.

'Yes, helping out at the Youth Club. You ought to see her on the snooker table. She even beat David.'

Sal reported her findings to the gang. The next Sunday found them all just happening to be walking down the street, as people wandered along to church.

'She's there,' said Cowboy, pointing to a smartly clad figure striding purposefully along. As they watched, Miss Winter turned into the church porch and disappeared from view. What would happen next?

The gang hung around until the service ended. Their patience was rewarded. At last, after everyone else had left the church and stood in little knots cluttering up the pavement, they appeared.

'They're holding hands!' squealed Cowboy. 'Look!'

And so they were.

'But he's a vicar . . .' began Tag.

'A curate . . .' corrected Sal.

'Well, a curate then . . . they don't hold hands!'

'Well, this one does,' said Sal from her vantage point in the newsagent's doorway.

'Must be in love,' smiled Narrinder. 'Isn't it nice?' She loved soppy things and even cried at the old black and white films on TV.

'Wait 'til we tell everyone,' said Tag. 'I'm going home now. Dinner time. Mission Accomplished.'

There wasn't much point in following them any more so Sal spent most of the next week at Narrinder's. Even then they got bored.

'Tell you what,' said Sal, one day as the rain streamed down Narrinder's bedroom window. 'Let's do another project.'

'Oh no,' groaned her friend, rolling off her bed where

she had been lying on her stomach, reading through a pile of old comics. 'I couldn't. Not again!'

'No, not like the last one. Just drawings. On paper. Go on, Narrinder. It'd be something to do.'

Narrinder smiled at her friend and agreed. It was hard not to. Sal looked so serious, even dressed up in Narrinder's best sari which was falling down at the waist.

So they decided to do a huge drawing with everything about Easter all on one sheet of paper. The Jesus bit got squashed up next to rabbits, chickens and eggs. Daffodils and tulips made a decorative border and the whole thing took them hours.

'We'll give it to Miss Winter, when we go back,' said Sal 'She's sure to think that it's great. It'll make up for the other one.'

'She might even give us an Easter egg,' suggested Narrinder. 'They're selling them cheap now that Easter is over!'

'Doubt it, but it's worth a try.'

As it turned out, it was worth a try. Miss Winter seemed genuinely pleased.

'Well, you two,' she said early on the first morning of term, 'I can see that you have been working very hard. Let's have a good look.' She paused and examined the drawing in detail. 'This is certainly creative, original . . . and thought out. And best of all, it doesn't smell!' She smiled at them both.

'Can we have a prize?' Sal asked.

'Well, no. The competition is over.' Seeing their crestfallen faces, Miss came up with an idea. 'I'll tell you what, I was going to take the projects down today, to make room for this term's work. Instead, we'll leave them up until the end of the week and put yours there as well. Okay?'

'Oh yes, Miss, thanks,' said both girls. Really, Miss Winter wasn't that bad after all, thought Sal. She hated it when people went on and on about things she'd done weeks ago. Like Dad and Boss. She would never hear the end of the youth club dance, and the washing machine. I mean, she hadn't known that the bubble stuff would clog up the works and that the repair man would charge Mum pounds to fix it. At least Miss Winter might not keep reminding them of the disastrous project.

Sal felt really happy that morning, for the first time in weeks. School was okay. The gang could have fun at break times. They had decided to make secret codes and have a club.

'It's just for us four,' insisted Sal at lunch. 'No one else, or it won't work.'

'Not even Brian and Vicki?' asked Tag. 'I mean, Brian's okay. He's let me have loads of goes on his computer.'

'You've *played* with him?' Sal was outraged.

'Yes. He only lives around the corner. He's really good on the computer. It's in his spare room. He's got hundreds of games.'

'But I said they're not to be in the gang,' Sal emphasised, looking fierce.

'Well, I like him,' Tag for once stood his ground.

Sal was stumped. If they had Brian, then they'd end up having Vicki. She'd rather die than see that happen.

'At home you can do what you like,' she finally compromised, 'but at school it's just us four. Okay?'

Narrinder, Cowboy and Tag nodded solemnly and Sal heaved a sigh of relief. Why they kept wanting creeps like Brian and Vicki was beyond her. Still, she had got her way this time. Little did she know that it would be the last time that she would ever get her own way again.

Feeling happy, Sal lined up with class 3N as the bell rang out for the start of afternoon lessons. Even the sight of Vicki did not bother her. It was fine. She was in control.

So Sal quickly hung up her coat and hurried into the classroom, eager to get ready for PE which was always fun. She found her shorts and gym shirt and struggled into her tight pumps unaware that in the next few minutes something would happen that would change her life.

8

'Right, sit down, all of you,' called Miss Winter. 'Register, before PE.'

The roomful of squirming bodies was noisily transformed as the class found their own seats. Most of them were still half-dressed.

'You can finish getting changed, in a minute,' boomed Miss Winter, as the din settled.

She went over to her desk and sat down. And then it happened. She was on the floor. Still. Not moving, lying awkwardly, half on top of her fallen chair.

A couple of children on the front row stood up and moved forward, uncertain what to do. The rest sat silently for what seemed hours, but was only a few seconds.

'It's Miss,' said Brian, somewhat unnecessarily. 'It's Miss.'

Miss moaned softly as a few of the children dashed down the corridor to the next classroom. They brought Mr Page back with them and then things happened very quickly.

Tag was sent to get the Head, Mrs Preston, and when she arrived she summoned the class into the hall, under the watchful eye of old Page. He tried to get them to 'move to music' but it was hopeless. They were too excited, talking all at once.

'What happened?'

'Brian did you see . . .'

'Why did she fall?'

'I'm frozen. I've only got my vest on . . .'

'Sir, is Miss all right?'

Mr Page gave up trying to teach them. He was a small nervous man who always wore a shiny black suit to school. He looked as if he should have retired years ago. The tape that was urging them to 'be like little seeds, growing, growing into shoots, and flowers' was turned off.

'I don't know what has happened,' he said. 'Miss Winter seems to have fallen and bumped her head. I don't know why.'

His own class came into the hall to join them, shepherded by the school secretary, who looked totally harrassed. She and Mr Page did not appear to be too pleased to have the combined forces of 3N and 3F to deal with.

'Sir, sir,' It was Cowboy, trying to make himself heard. 'It was the chair. The leg was broken. All smashed like.'

Mr Page listened at last. 'Broken?'

'Yes, sir,' Rachel, who sat on the front row so she could see the blackboard through her thick glasses, answered. 'It weren't her usual chair, sir.'

'Wasn't, not weren't,' Mr Page corrected her automatically.

'Well it weren't anyway,' Rachel carried on, aware that everyone was listening to her. 'Her chair has got a rip by the corner of the seat. I ought to know, I sits right by it.'

A babble of sound broke out, stray phrases floated into the general hub-bub.

'Course it was her chair.'

'Will Miss be teaching us tomorrow?'

'Rachel's as blind as a bat.'

'Can I fetch my jumper, sir?'

The general noise ceased abruptly. An ambulance drove past the hall's full length windows. Over sixty pairs of eyes watched silently, as two ambulance men disappeared and then returned, carrying a stretcher with someone draped in a red blanket on it.

'It's Miss,' wailed a voice.

'They're red, so you can't see the blood,' explained Brian, but no one was listening. 'The blankets.'

'Is she dead?' Narrinder's eyes were full of tears, as she hung on to Sal's arm.

Just then Mrs Preston sailed into the room and silence fell. She was a large, imposing woman, who walked very upright. As usual she was wearing a skirt and blouse, this time white, with frills cascading down her ample front.

'Well, children,' she began, managing to look as if she could see right inside them when she talked. 'Miss Winter has had an unfortunate accident. She banged her head when she fell off the chair. It's not too serious, although she has gone to hospital. Anyone with a head injury has to be checked over.' She turned to Mr Page. 'Well, Mr Page, what are you going to do with all these for the rest of the afternoon?'

Mr Page blinked. Before he could come up with an answer, Mrs Preston gave him one.

'The video, I think. Last Christmas's performance of "Alice in Wonderland" should get us through until home time.'

As Sal got dressed, she couldn't help but think about Miss Winter.

Why had she fallen? I mean she wasn't old or anything, yet she'd gone down so quickly. And after she'd been nice to her and Narrinder! It didn't make sense. It wasn't fair.

Fortunately the video, which was hilarious, soon stopped the children worrying about their teacher. The

48

sight of Tom as the Cheshire cat, complete with fur cat's head, that looked as if it had been mauled by a lion, had them smiling. When the Red Queen's (Paul's) dress split in the disco dancing scene, even old Page laughed.

'Like your boxer shorts!' called out Tom.

'Lovely legs!'

'Such a pretty dress.' That was from Tag.

'Shut up,' shouted Paul. 'Wait until the finale!'

That was when the scenery, well, the cardboard castle cut-out, had collapsed, sending the tree, alias Peter from 3F, head first into the audience.

They all laughed, the tension of the early afternoon broken. Mr Page re-ran the final scene four times until the bell sounded to go home.

As they struggled out into the watery sunshine of early spring, everyone was talking about what had happened.

'Perhaps it was a different chair,' suggested Narrinder to Sal as they made their way to the shop.

'But that doesn't make sense,' said Sal, 'Why should she have a different chair?'

'Rachel could have got it wrong.'

'She doesn't usually.'

'Well, it's a real mystery. We could solve it in the club. Come on Sal, race you to the shop,' and Narrinder set off, leaving Sal to plod along behind.

It was a mystery, but by the time they had got to school the next day, it was well on the way to being solved.

They had assembly straight away. Mrs Preston droned on about something. Sal wasn't listening. She was staring at the person at the end of the row.

'Who's that?' she whispered to Tag.

'Supply teacher. Tom told me. His mum knows the school secretary. She's taking us.'

Sal stared even harder at the apparition. She was wearing tight black trousers which disappeared into black boots, above this was a huge black fluffy sweater and perched on top of that, was a tiny doll's face with clouds of black frizzy hair. Great, dangling black and silver earrings hung from somewhere under the hair. Auden Junior School had never seen anything like it.

Sal was pulled back to the present by the sound of Mrs Preston '. . . and so she will be resting at home for a couple of days. Miss Lorelli will be taking her class until she comes back.'

Class 3N dashed back to their room, eager for a closer look at Miss Lorelli, who wafted this wonderful smell around her. Sal, however, wasn't to get much time to look.

'Good morning. I'm Miss Lorelli and I'm going to be teaching you for a few days. Now before we begin is there a . . .' she paused and looked at a slip of paper in her hand. '. . . a Sally Musgrove here this morning?'

Sally raised her hand.

'Ah, Sally. You are to go straight to Mrs Preston's office. At once. 'Miss Lorelli sounded very stern. In fact her big voice didn't sound like it came from such a small body.

'Mrs Preston's?' Sal's voice shook. There must be some mistake. You only went to Mrs Preston for one of two reasons. Either you had done a piece of brilliant work. It couldn't be that. Or you'd done something really awful. And it couldn't be that. Or could it? Not the egg business. Surely not. That was over and done with. Or was it?

Sal felt totally sick as she walked along the corridor. What had she done? Taking a deep breath, she pulled her socks up, attempted to straighten her skirt and button up her cardigan. With a trembling hand she knocked on the door and waited for the dreaded summons to enter.

9

'Come in.'

Sal opened the door slowly and walked into the room. Uncertain what to do, she stood near Mrs Preston's desk and waited.

Mrs Preston looked at her for what seemed to be hours. Sal lowered her own eyes. She didn't like what she saw. Mrs Preston sat there like a carved statue. Her perfectly groomed hair was like a cap above her pinky skin and piercing slate grey eyes. She folded her wrinkled hands together on the desk top and, after pulling down the sleeves on her green silk blouse, began to speak.

'Well, Sally,' she began. 'I'm afraid that I've got to ask you some questions.' She paused. 'And I want the truth. Do you understand?' Sal nodded, nervously picking little strands of fluff from her cardigan and rolling them into a ball. What questions?

'It's about yesterday. Miss Winter's accident. We know for certain that her chair was removed and a broken one, out of the store cupboard, put in its place. At lunch-time most likely,' Mrs Preston looked straight at her, not that Sal realised. She was staring at the hexagonal patterns on the carpet.

'Sally, look at me. Did you have anything to do with the broken chair?'

'Oh, no, Mrs Preston. Course not.' Sal was so relieved

that the words came out in a tumble. Thank goodness this was one thing she had nothing to do with. Phew – no trouble after all!

'Are you sure?'

'Yes, Mrs Preston.' Sal looked up at her. 'I was playing out at lunch-time. Anyway I like Miss Winter. I didn't want her to get hurt.'

'Didn't want her to get hurt? That rather sounds to me, Sally, as though you knew about the chair before the accident.'

'No, no I didn't. I just meant that . . . that I didn't know anything about it. Honest.' Sal stumbled to a halt. The more she said the less convincing it sounded. Surely Mrs Preston couldn't believe that *she'd* done it.

'Honest?' queried the Headteacher, picking up on Sal's last word. 'I'm afraid, Sally, that I'm not convinced of your honesty. I'm well aware of what happened to the lunch-boxes, and on April Fool's Day – strange that no one owned up for that, wasn't it?'

Sal said nothing.

'Sally, were you responsible for those . . . those happenings?'

It was no use. She would have to confess, otherwise she'd be in even more trouble. Goodness knew what the result of owning up would be.

'But, Mrs Preston, they were only tricks.'

'So, you *did* do them?'

'Yes, but only for a laugh. Honest.'

Mrs Preston stood up and came towards Sal.

'And I suppose that yesterday's episode was only for a laugh, as well, wasn't it?'

'*No*,' Sal was nearly shouting. 'I never did it! It wasn't me!'

'Sally, when are you going to stop lying?' Mrs Preston gently took hold of her arm. Sal tried unsuccessfully to shake it off.

'I'm *not* lying,' she said desperately, her face just inches from the head's heaving bosom. What could she say to convince Mrs Preston of her innocence? It was like a trial. And for something she hadn't done!

Mrs Preston moved away and seemed to be gazing at an old oil painting of a ship on the wall.

'Sally, you were seen going into the library at lunchtime. The store cupboard leads off the library. The broken chair was in the store cupboard. The library is out of bounds at lunch-time. How do you explain that?'

That was easy enough. 'I wanted to take out the next book in the "Secret Seven" series. So did Tom. So I went to hide it in the library, so he couldn't find it before me when we change our books. That's all.'

'Well, in that case you can show me where you hid it.'

'But, Mrs Preston, I couldn't find it so I couldn't hide it, but I did look.' As she was speaking Sal knew that Mrs Preston did not believe her. It was no use answering her or trying to argue back. Mrs Preston had made up her mind.

'Sally,' she said. 'I don't believe you. I think that you exchanged the chairs, for a joke, a laugh. I accept that you didn't mean to hurt Miss Winter, but the fact remains, that you did. Now I'm going to give you one more opportunity to own up. Sally, did you swop the chairs around?'

'No.' Sal's cheeks were burning like fire. She could not stop fidgeting. Her eyes were downcast and inside she felt like she had died. Mrs Preston did not believe her. No one else would believe her either. This was awful, terrible. What would happen next?

Mrs Preston looked at the miserable girl in front of her, and saw all the obvious signs of guilt. She flicked through a card index in a cold, grey filing cabinet.

'I'm going to phone your mother. In the meantime go

and wait outside this room.'

Obediently Sal left the room and collapsed onto the hard wooden chair in the corridor. She rested her head on her hands, her elbows on her scuffed knees. Never before had she felt so alone, so dreadful inside. She had been accused of a crime she had not committed! Hot, salty tears began to trickle unchecked down her red face, forming droplets that splashed gently off the end of her freckled chin. She sat there for ages. The bell for break sounded and she could hear the excited shouting, and stamping feet of hordes of children let loose for fifteen minutes.

Just as the bell for the end of break sounded, Sal heard a thumping and scraping at the big double doors that opened into the corridor. She shifted her position and looked up. It was Mum! She looked mad. Desperately Mum rammed the doors with the double buggy she was pushing and stormed into the corridor. One small 'littly' hung onto her anorak pocket while Lizzie and another baby bawled their heads off in the buggy.

'Watch this lot,' said Mum, looking at Sal so fiercely that Sal discovered that it was possible to feel even worse than she already did.

Mum barged into Mrs Preston's office without even knocking. The 'littly' took off his wellies and went to investigate the plant stand, pulling leaves off a trailing ivy. Lizzie stopped crying and tried to get out of the buggy. Frustrated in her efforts by the network of the straps, she yelled 'Out! Out!' so loudly that the school secretary appeared to see what was going on. She ended up watching the three 'littlies' and telling Sal that it was all her fault.

Just then Mum reappeared. If she'd looked mad before she looked like she would blow up now.

'Get your anorak! Get outside! Follow me!' she hissed as she collected the 'littlies', retrieving one wellington boot out of a plant pot, and pushed her way out of the doors.

When Mum was mad she always did things fast, like walking and talking. Sal had to half run to keep up with her, as she swept off down the road, pushing the buggy into the biting wind, and dragging the other 'littly' behind her. She was shouting so fast that Sal could only make out odd phrases.

'Never felt so humiliated in all my life . . . wait 'til I get hold of you . . . Lizzie wasn't even dressed . . . I just don't know what I'm going to do . . . What do you think you were playing at . . . Just wait until your dad gets home . . .'

When she ran out of what to say, Mum went back to the beginning, hardly pausing for breath. She's like one of Boss's new records, thought Sal, playing the same tune, over and over again.

By the time Mum had unloaded all the children into the hallway at home, Sal was certain of some facts. One, Mrs Preston still blamed her for the accident. Two, so did Mum. Three, she wasn't half going to get 'it' whatever 'it' was, when Mum calmed down. Four, she'd got to stay off school till Monday and then she had to sit at a desk, on her own, at the front of the class. And all for something she had not done! The unfairness of it all sliced through her thin, wiry body like a knife.

'Sally, come here,' Mum was in the kitchen, having shut the door on the 'littlies' in the living room. Sal came. Mum was trying to calm down, but not doing a very good job of it. Her hair was sticking up like candy-floss as Mum ran her hands through it in exasperation.

'I'm up to here with you,' she said, indicating her neck. 'I thought you'd learned, "no more tricks", you said. You little liar . . .'

'I'm *not* a liar,' interrupted Sal. 'I *didn't* do it!

'Didn't do it? Don't come that one with me. What do

you think I felt like, struggling to school with all that lot in there, to be told that my daughter, that *you*, were a liar and a trouble causer . . .'

'But Mum. I *didn't* . . .'

'Shut up,' Mum screamed. 'Get to your room, and stay there before I do something I'll regret. You ever show me up like that again, Sally Musgrove, and you'll wish you'd never been born.'

10

Sal had to stay in her room most of the time until Monday came around. She was almost relieved to be going back to school. It could not be much worse than being at home, where no one believed her and everyone treated her as if she had got the plague.

However, her relief did not last long.

'Hello,' she shouted, dashing into the shop, 'Where's Narrinder?'

Narrinder's mum, who was on the till, glanced up. 'Oh, she's gone. Vicki called for her, about ten minutes ago.'

Vicki! Called for Narrinder! What on earth was happening. Sal ran as fast as she could to school and into the playground. Ignoring Vicki, she pushed in front of Narrinder.

'Why didn't you wait for me? You always do.'

'Not any more,' replied Narrinder. 'Vicki calls for me now. You can call as well, if you like.'

Sal didn't like, not if Vicki was there as well. She pulled Narrinder to one side.

'What's this with you and Vicki? You're my friend, not hers.'

'She's okay, Sal. She has some good ideas. When you were away last week, we all had some good fun together.'

'All?'

'Me and Vicki, Tag and Cowboy, and Brian.'

'But the club, the gang . . .' began Sal.

'Well, it wasn't the same without you, so we let them join. We've worked out some secret codes. Brian's brought his walkie-talkie. Tag's mum says she'll send us some buns.' In her enthusiasm to tell Sal of their plans, Narrinder did not notice the expression on Sal's face. It was *her* club, *her* gang. How dare they make plans without her!

Worse was to come. At morning break, the gang met at their usual place, second bin on the left, by the nearly dead birch tree.

'Your name's Las,' said Tag.

'Las?'

'Yup, code you see. It's Sal, backwards. I'm Gat, he's Yobwoc, she's Ran, Narrinder was too long to do it all. She's Civ and he's Nairb,' Tag finished, pointing to Vicki and Brian.

'But they're not in it,' said Sal.

'We want them,' stated Tag. 'We're fed up of you bossing us around.'

'We sorted it out last week,' said Cowboy, alias Yobwoc. 'Is it true that you swopped the chairs?'

'Course not.'

'But everyone says it was you.'

'That's why you were off.'

'Weren't. I had a cold.' Sal quickly fibbed.

'But why do you have to sit at the front then?'

'Ears.'

'Ears?'

'Gone funny. After the cold.' Sal was having to think fast.

'You idiot. You're a lying toad!' Tag was learning to assert himself. 'We know you did it.'

'I didn't,' Sal stamped her feet angrily. She always seemed to be saying 'I didn't' these days. Surely the gang believed her. They had to. 'You believe me, don't you?'

Her question was answered by silence. With mounting disbelief, Sal looked around at her friends, and enemies. Tag and Cowboy looked sullen. It didn't matter what Vicki and Brian thought, but Narrinder, her best friend Narrinder. She must believe her.

'Narrinder . . . ?' she pleaded, but Narrinder turned her head.

'I'd like to believe you, Sal!' she began, 'but who else would have done it? It had to be you.' Pain knotted up Sal's stomach. No one, not even Narrinder, believed her. She wanted the playground to open and swallow her up. Swiftly her hurt turned to anger.

'Well, you lot can get lost. I don't need you. Or your stupid club. Or your grotty codes and barmy games.' Sal turned and stamped off as far away from them as she could, determined that they would not see the tears of rage and hurt that were pouring down her face.

She ran and locked herself in the outside toilet. Sitting on the loo seat, she noisily blew her nose on about a metre of toilet roll – the scratchy sort that just leaves your nose red and sore. She'd show them. She needed no one. That Narrinder could take a running jump, for all she cared. But at the same time that she felt so cross, Sal also felt terribly sad. There seemed to be another voice inside her. One that said it was awful. It was so unfair, so wrong. Punished by Mum and Dad, convicted by Mrs Preston, and now, even worse, rejected by her friends. There was nobody, nobody in the whole world who knew how she felt. Nobody could help her. Nobody cared.

The rest of the morning passed very slowly. Convinced that the class were watching her, Sal worked out a way of writing 'What I did over the weekend' with her head down, cradled in her arms. Not that she had much to write, being stuck in her tiny, scruffy bedroom most of the time. She invented a trip to town and a visit to McDonald's. At least it took time to write it.

As soon as the lunch bell sounded, Miss Winter, who had recovered now, asked Sal to wait behind.

'I understand that you didn't mean me to get hurt,' she began. Sal decided that there was no point in protesting her innocence, yet again. 'I trust that you've learned your lesson.'

Sal nodded solemnly.

'Well, after you've had your sandwiches, I want you to come in here and work. We need to get the stained glass picture off the window. You can do it at break, as well.'

Sal nodded and felt relieved. At least she wouldn't be out in the playground, alone.

So, ten minutes later, Sal was wrestling with the faded and frayed picture on the window. The black tape was still as sticky as tar. Pity she hadn't used it on the egg project. Tearing the scraps of paper off the glass, Sal found her mind wandering. Here were the soldiers Tag and Cowboy had done. They'd all been happy then. Well, she had been, at any rate. And now? It was so unfair, unjust. That sounded better. Unjust. Wasn't that what Miss had said about the Easter story? Something about Jesus and it being unjust.

Violently she tore across the tissue paper. It was the bit with the hill and the crosses. If this Jesus was interested in what was fair, he wouldn't have let it happen. Not to him. Not to her. I mean, he let them nail him to a cross. How could he? It must have been terrible.

She rolled up the sticky papers and threw them in the direction of the bin. Missed. Anyway, if Jesus was God, and God knew everything and God was love, why did things happen that weren't fair? And that bit about love. Miss had said that Jesus had died because he loved people. Well, if he loved her, why had he let her get

60

into trouble?

'It's your fault,' she muttered aloud to the tattered remains of the Easter story. 'You shouldn't have let it happen. Why did you let them hurt you? Why?' Tearing down the garden where Jesus had come alive again, she carried on. 'I mean, you came alive again. It worked out all right. But, God, wherever you are, what about me? How can it work out all right?' Her muttering ended in a sob.

Slowly a thought began to form in Sal's mind. When she'd sat on the loo she'd known that nobody, yes nobody, understood her. Yet perhaps that wasn't true. Perhaps this Jesus did. After all he knew what it was like to be unfairly treated.

Sal continued to talk to herself. 'I'll pray to Jesus, like in assembly. Here goes. "Our Father who art in heaven" . . . well that's not much use, what does "art" mean, anyway?' She paused. 'Well, God, I'm so fed-up. I expect you were too, when Jesus died. Can you sort it out, like you did for him?' Sal wasn't quite satisfied. Her prayer did not sound posh enough, so she decided to finish it off, like they did in Assembly. 'For yours is the kingdom, the power and the glory, Amen, from Sally Musgrove.' There, God would know it was her prayer now. She wondered how he ever sorted out who was praying what. Perhaps he had this enormous computer in heaven, and pressed some buttons, and sent back the answers. She'd have to wait and see.

It was strange, really, but she felt a bit better now that she had talked to God. He did understand and if anyone could sort it all out, he could.

Somehow she got through the afternoon and finished cleaning the window at break. She scuttled out of the gate as fast as she could at home-time. Sal did not want anyone to see that she was alone with no one to walk with. She would go the long way round, as home wasn't that inviting.

Hands deep inside her anorak pockets, Sal whistled tunelessly along the drab streets, as she kicked a dented Coke can in front of her. She was re-living the events of the day. Bit like watching a video. She grinned. A horror video. Suddenly she stopped. It was something Narrinder had said. 'It had to be you. Who else would have done it?'

But it wasn't me, Sal's heart lightened. So, it must be someone else. All I've got to do, is to find out who it was. Then it will be okay. She turned, with a sense of purpose, into her street. That was it. Find out who did it.

11

It was one thing to decide to find out who had done it, but quite another to actually hunt out the real culprit.

Sal spent the evening working out her plans. She would have to be a detective, like on television. That meant she needed a kit, something for fingerprints, a notebook and a magnifying glass. The magnifying glass was a dead loss. The Musgrove household did not possess such a thing. She found a nearly clean notebook in among Grump's stuff. Ignoring the title 'Homework Record Book', she wrote 'The mystery of the broken chair' in purple felt-tip across the front.

Now for fingerprints. Mum's 'Eastern Passion Flower' talc would do to start with. Detectives always dusted things with white powder. Sal wasn't clear why but maybe she would work it out by the time she actually did it. Then she needed something black to stick fingers in, to make prints. It was a good job that her brothers were out, thought Sal, as she rummaged through their room. Ah, there it was. Boss's oil paints. She helped herself to a tube of black and one of dark brown. Locking the bathroom door, she set to work to make her mix. The result of blending oil paint, soap and a drop of water was interesting. Sal had mixed it in the soap dish, now to try it out.

Putting her fingers into the gooey mess, she pressed them onto the nearest thing, the tiled wall. Great! You could really see the shapes and whirls. She had another go, and another.

'Sal, what are you doing? Hurry up, it's Lizzie's bathtime.'

Mum! Sal realised what she was doing and stared at the wall. Hundreds of finger-marks, like puppy's paw-prints, walked all over the wall.

'Come on, Sally, open the door.'

'I'll bath her, Mum.' Sal shot out of the door, picked up Lizzie and was back in the bathroom at the speed of light.

'Me do,' said Lizzie, pointing to the art work.

'No, shush,' replied Sal, running the water and undressing her little sister at the same time. Oh heck, paint all over her clothes. Never mind, she'd turn them inside out later, when her hands were clean, so Mum would not notice.

Casually Sal wiped the wall with a cloth. No result. Using the nail-brush and the scouring powder, she began to make inroads into the tell-tale trellis of marks.

'Out,' stated Lizzie. 'Out.'

'No, you've got to stay there.'

'Out!' yelled Lizzie.

'Sal, have you finished?' Mum's voice floated up the stairs.

'Soon,' shouted Sal, and then turned to her sister and in a whisper said, 'Look, stay there, till I've finished.'

'Out!'

'I'll sing then,' and by the time Sal had exhausted her supply of nursery rhymes, the wall was clean. Lizzie, by now covered in goose-pimples, was heaved out of the cold water and Sal had just got her dry, as Mum stormed upstairs to see what was going on.

Retrieving the soap dish, and the ruined nail-brush, Sal reached the safety of her own room. Phew! That had been a close shave. Mum would have erupted if she had seen the mess.

There was only one thing left to do. Taking Grump's notebook, she listed all the suspects for the crime. The whole of her class, and 3F and a few teachers, dinner ladies and the caretaker thrown in for good measure. Then she drew some columns headed, 'Might have done it', 'Couldn't have done it', and 'Don't know'. Immensely satisfied by the evening's work, Sal drifted off to sleep, certain that by the same time tomorrow, all would be revealed.

Sal was waiting patiently in the playground at 8:17, for her classmates to arrive. Seeing Billy, of 3F, dawdling in with his mate Simon, she approached, flourished her four-coloured biro and notebook at them and began.

'Did you do it?'

'Do what?' asked Billy.

'Move Miss Winter's chair.'

'Don't be a wally.'

'How about you, Simon?'

'You're nuts, Sally Musgrove. Always have been,' and Simon and Billy drifted off.

Sal marked two red crosses in the 'Don't know' column by their names. Well the direct approach had not worked very well. She'd try something else. Ah, here were Vicki and Narrinder. I suppose I had better ask them, Sal thought. Here goes.

'Vicki! Narrinder!' Sal caught their attention and they turned towards her expectantly. 'Where were you on the night of last Tuesday.'

'The night of last Tuesday?'

'I mean, the dinner-time.'

'What are you playing at, Sal?'

'Just answer the questions,' replied Sal, copying her favourite detective by talking out of the side of her mouth. He always got the right replies.

'Don't be so daft. What are you up to?' asked Vicki.

'I've got to find out who did it,' stated Sal. 'It wasn't me, so it must be someone else. I'm a detective.'

'Defective, more like,' said Vicki, who liked to show off. 'It means stupid,' she explained to Narrinder. 'Come on, here's the rest of the gang.' and they left Sal with just two more red crosses in the 'Don't know' column, for her efforts.

By the end of the day, Sal had questioned nearly everyone. The 'Don't know' column was full of red marks and there were three yellow ticks in the 'couldn't have done it' column. They were Miss Winter, who Sal had decided probably had not planned to bump her own head, Peter Wilkins who was at home with chicken-pox and Jayne Martin, who was a right baby, and had taken the whole day off just to go to the dentist.

A bit disappointed by her results, Sal cheered herself up with the thought that there were still the fingerprints left to do.

So the following lunch time found Sal pretending to be working hard in the library. Miss Winter had given her permission to stay in to copy up the work she had missed. There was no one else around. Now for it.

Stealthily, Sal crept over to the store cupboard. Half hidden under discarded costumes from the Christmas play, and huge sheets of card, was the chair. Sal pulled it out, sending the card clanging to the floor, making a din that was bound to be heard. Sal tensed and listened. Sighing with relief, she got to work, unaware that a purple cloak worn by the chief king in the nativity play was draped over her back.

I'll just puff the powder over it, thought Sal, squirting 'Eastern Passion Flower' in great clouds around herself. Now, I'll find the prints. She drew the chair nearer. Aw, this is hopeless. Where do I begin? I can't see anything. It's not like this on the telly!

She squatted back on her heels, staring at the chair,

waiting for inspiration. Engrossed in her detecting, she did not hear the soft approach of footsteps.

Miss Winter stood, framed in the store cupboard doorway, staring in amazement at the sight before her. A ginger-haired child, on her knees, covered in an old curtain, surrounded by a white dust cloud, that smelt like bathtime. Suddenly the talc made Miss Winter sneeze.

Sal shot upright and turned, her way of escape barred by the teacher. Her heart began to race, and she clenched her fists tightly, as the blood drained from her already pale face. Gosh, this was awful. She was already in trouble. Miss Winter would go berserk.

'Sally Musgrove, what on earth are you doing?'

Sal kept quiet. This was going to take some explaining.

'This is a funny way to catch up on your work.'

Sal looked up. Miss was smiling! Encouraged by this, Sal plunged headlong into a jumbled explanation.

'It's the chair. I've got to get the fingerprints. It wasn't me that did it. I'm a detective . . . but it won't work. I can't find them, and no one believes me . . .' Sal stumbled to a halt.

Miss Winter looked at her thoughtfully. Was this another trick? Or was there just a chance that Sal was genuine, that she was telling the truth?

'Sally,' she said slowly. 'Is this another of your tricks?'

'Oh, no, Miss. I'm telling the truth. I am. Really.' Sal wanted Miss to believe her. Please, God, she thought, help her to believe me. Please. I can't stand it, if she doesn't.

'Sit down, Sal,' said Miss Winter, perching on one of the library tables. 'Is this what this is all about as well?' Miss had got her notebook. 'You left it on your desk. I see that you crossed me off your suspect list.'

Sal was confused. Miss Winter was being kind to her.

Yet she was the one who had got injured. Everyone else was horrible, but Miss seemed to be listening. She would try, once more, to prove her innocence.

'I didn't do it, Miss.'

Miss Winter looked straight at her. 'You know, Sally, I'm beginning to wonder if it was you after all. I've forgiven you for doing it, but maybe you are the wrong person to forgive. I don't suppose we'll ever really know, unless someone owns up, will we?'

'No, Miss, but I can't own up, can I, when it wasn't me?' Sal felt like dancing. At last someone almost thought that she was telling the truth.

'You can clear up the mess in there,' Miss Winter indicated the storeroom, 'and then go. I need to think about all this.'

Sal made the clearing up last until the end of the lunch break. There was hope after all. Miss might believe her. Then everything would be all right. I'll even make friends with Vicki, she thought, if it all gets sorted out.

12

Just before the end of the afternoon, Miss Winter got the children's attention and began to talk.

'It's exactly one week ago today that we had the accident, here in the classroom. I want to talk to you all about it.'

What was she going to say, thought Sal, squirming in her chair, while curling and uncurling her toes inside her old grey trainers. She had had enough of the chair incident. Was Miss Winter going to tell everyone that Sally Musgrove hadn't done it?

'I expect that most of you know that a certain person was blamed for swopping the chairs,' continued the teacher.

Sal felt the entire class staring at her. She just carried on looking at the ink marks and carved notches on her desk top. That one at the top was like a map of Australia.

'However I am not convinced that Sally Musgrove was responsible.'

A hum of voices grew into a loud babble.

'But, Miss, the Head thought it was her.'

'She had to stay off school.'

'Course it was her, always doing tricks.'

'What about the lunch-boxes?'

'And April Fools?'

'Be quiet,' Miss Winter calmed the excited class. 'I think, that perhaps someone else caused the accident.'

'Someone else!'

'Weren't me, Miss!'

'Who?'

'I don't know who. I don't even know if it was someone else. However, if it was any one of you,' Miss Winter's eyes travelled over each child in the room, 'any one of you,' she repeated, 'I want to give you the opportunity to tell me. It's very wrong to let someone else get into trouble, when they haven't done something. I'll stay behind, in here, after school, each night this week, in case one of you wants to tell me something.'

The class were stunned. Not Sal! Then who could it be. Only Sal would have dared to do that! No one else had the nerve. It had to be Sal.

First thing the next morning, Sal was at Miss Winter's desk, her unspoken question showing in her face.

'I'm afraid not, Sally,' Miss Winter said kindly. 'No one wanted to see me after school last night.'

Sal went dejectedly to her desk. Perhaps tomorrow? But tomorrow the answer was just the same.

At least the gang had let her join them again. Well, sort of join them. They did not take too much notice of her ideas.

'Can we all be detectives?' said Sal, at break. 'Find out who did it?'

'No, it's daft,' replied Tag.

'Daft, Why?'

'Well, you didn't get very far, doing your detecting.'

'Even heard that you asked the dinner ladies,' chuckled Cowboy. 'Can't imagine them bopping Winter on the head.'

'If you all helped, we'd find out,' Sal tried to win them over to her viewpoint. 'All detectives have partners. Sherlock Holmes and Watson. Poirot and Hastings.'

'Laurel and Hardy?' queried Tag, whose dad was into old movies.

'Tom and Jerry?'

'Yogi Bear and Boo-Boo?'

'No, seriously, we could all find out,' said Sal.

'No,' Vicki's voice cut into the conversation. 'We all still think you did it, anyway. Miss Winter's mad to believe your story.'

Sal glanced at Vicki. She looked quite worked up, almost angry. Strange. Sal still did not like her, but when it came to the choice between no friends, or the gang plus Vicki, Sal felt she had no option.

The next morning, which was Friday, Sal went across to Miss Winter's desk.

'Any news?' she asked eagerly, although she did not really expect an answer. She noticed that the teacher had had her highlights done again. Looked quite pretty.

'After assembly, Mrs Preston wants to see you.'

'Why?'

'She'll tell you.' Sal had to be satisfied with that. All through assembly, Sal watched Mrs Preston, who carried on about litter in the playground. What was she going to say to her? It was impossible to tell from the look on her face. Why did she want to see her again? What was it all about?

Half an hour later Sal once more found herself outside the Head's study. Her stomach was in tight knots and she wished she had put her clean shirt on, not this one with the hot chocolate stain on it. To her surprise, there was someone else waiting outside the door. A tall, smartly dressed girl, in shining black patent shoes, whose head hung down as if she was studying the floor. Her shoulder-length straight glossy hair almost hid her face.

'Vicki!' gasped Sal. 'What are you doing here?'

Vicki made no reply. I expect she's done another piece of brilliant work, thought Sal, I bet Brian helped her. Mind you, where was it?

At that moment the door opened. A grim faced Mrs Preston beckoned them.

'Both of us?' asked Sal. 'At the same time?'

'I want to see you together,' said the Head. 'Now sit down here,' indicating two chairs. 'Vicki would you please tell me and Sally what you told Miss Winter last night.'

Sal's mind was whirling. What she told Miss Winter? Vicki! Vicki? She couldn't have . . . not her . . . she'd never have . . .

'Come along, Vicki,' Mrs Preston loomed above them, her strong voice sounding out of place in this small room.

'It was me. I swopped the chairs.' Vicki's voice was soft and she was mumbling into her jumper so that Sal wasn't sure she had heard correctly.

'You what?'

'I did it. Me,' Vicki looked straight at her.

For once Sal was lost for words. She was cleared! Someone else had done it. Someone else called Vicki! Vicki, who never did anything wrong, was, in Sal's opinion, a teacher's pet, and was such a goody goody. It couldn't be.

Mrs Preston seemed quite calm about it all.

'It was very brave of you to own up,' she said, 'but why did you do it? It's not like you at all!'

'I thought they'd like me. The gang. If I did a trick. I wanted to be in the gang. And show them I'd got some ideas, and I'm not chicken. I never knew that Miss would get hurt. I just thought they'd all laugh. But it all went wrong . . .' her voice tailed off as she sniffed loudly.

'But not to own up. To let someone else take your punishment.' Mrs Preston sounded perplexed. 'Can't you see that's wrong?'

'Yes, Mrs Preston.' Vicki turned to look at Sal. 'But when I knew it was only her, I didn't care. She was rotten to me. I hate her. The others would have let me join the gang, but not her. It served her right.'

Sal had never heard Vicki say so much at one go. To think she'd done it to join the gang! And much more importantly, to think that she had let her, Sally Musgrove, suffer for it. Sal had never liked Vicki but, all of a sudden, she knew what it was like to feel hate. How dare she! She'd sat there for a week, no, more than that, joined the gang and been happy because Sal was in trouble. She'd get her back, she'd show her, the big fat blob, if it was the last thing she ever did.

Mrs Preston was talking to her now, 'Sally, I'm sorry that we did not believe your story. I apologise. And I want you to realise that it was very hard for Vicki to confess. Very hard. So I'm sure you'll be able to forgive and forget and be friends.'

Some chance! thought Sal. Forgive that moron, she'd die first. Better not tell Mrs Preston that!

'And Vicki, I'll have to telephone your mother and you will have to have the same punishment that Sal had.'

Good, thought Sal. I hope everyone hates her.

Mrs Preston smiled at her. Although Sal was thinking hateful thoughts, she had her angelic face on, with the lopsided grin.

'Well, Sally, I think we can say that justice has been done. You must have felt very unfairly treated . . .', you bet, thought Sal, 'but I'm sure that we can all come out of this incident wiser and better.'

Not another lecture, Sal inwardly groaned, taking pleasure in Vicki's obvious embarrassment.

'So, Miss Winter will tell the class what has happened . . . And I want you two to be friends and forgive one another. Now Sally, off you go back to class. Vicki wait here.'

Sal leaped high into the air as soon as she was outside the room. She was free! This is what it must feel like to be released from prison. 'Yippee!' she yelled, jumping up again, trying to reach the ceiling. 'It wasn't me! It's all right!'

She burst into her classroom, grinning from ear to ear. 'It was Vicki!' she interrupted. 'Mrs Preston says so.'

The class once again fixed their eyes on her. Miss Winter briefly explained what had happened and they settled down to solving today's maths exercise.

Sal felt great. Yet deep down inside her was a growing determination. She'd get even with that Vicki. There was no doubt about it.

13

At lunch-time the gang all met in the playground.

'Fancy it being Vicki!' exclaimed Tag.

'I'm sorry I didn't believe you, Sal,' said Narrinder. 'Really I am. Let's be friends, like we used to be.' Her brown eyes looked solemnly at her old friend.

'Course,' Sal was excited. She grabbed Narrinder and swung her round so fast that the girls ended up in a giggling heap on the ground. Tag and Cowboy joined in laughing, all oblivious of the dust that was covering them.

Sitting up, Sal saw a pair of big black shoes, spindly legs encased in grey trousers, and as her gaze wandered upwards, it came to rest on Brian's bright blue eyes.

'What are you doing? Clear off.'

'Hang on a minute, Sal, he's okay. He's part of the gang,' said Tag.

'Not any longer.'

'But why?'

'Cos I say so.'

'Well I say so – that he is. If you'd not been rotten to him and Vicki, all this fuss would never have happened.' Tag disentangled himself and went to stand by Brian.

'What do you mean?' Sal was getting cross. Surely the others didn't still want Brian and Vicki.

'You wouldn't let them join. We didn't mind. You're too bossy.' Tag did not know what else to say.

Sal was unsure what to do. She had been positive that everything would go back to how it had been before Miss Winter's accident. Now it looked as if she was wrong.

'But you can't have *her* – Vicki,' said Sal. 'I mean, she did it.'

'We had you when we thought you'd done it,' replied Narrinder.

'That was different.'

'Why?'

'Well, it was, that's all.'

'Because it was *you*, not Vicki?' asked Narrinder. 'I don't see why she can't be part of the club. She's nice, really.'

'Nice! After what she did to me. You must be joking.'

'Well, we want them, whatever you say,' Cowboy was actually standing up for himself. 'This is stupid talk. Let's forget it and be friends.'

Sal gave up. So, the gang wanted Vicki. They could have her. She would pretend that she didn't mind. She was good at that. Pretending. Yet, inside, she would come up with a way of getting even with that creep. She would do it on her own, without the help of the gang. No one was going to get the better of her, if she could help it.

That afternoon, as she turned into her street, Sal saw something quite out of the ordinary. Mum was standing on the front doorstep, looking up the road. Could she be waiting for her? She was. As soon as Sal got within earshot, she began.

'Oh, Sal, I'm so glad it wasn't you. Mrs Preston phoned. And you'd been punished as well. I always knew it couldn't have been you . . .'

Not quite what she'd said! thought Sal.

'I said to Mrs Preston, that I always knew my girl was innocent, all along . . .'

Who was she kidding? Why had she made her stay in her room most of the time? Sal smiled to herself. Really, Mum was nuts expecting her to believe this lot.

'Anyway, let's take your coat,' Mum gave her a moist kiss. 'Now, I've got a little surprise. A celebration.' Sal followed in amazement. Mum was usually too tired to notice that she existed after school. All this attention was quite nice.

'Sit down and look.' In a large paper bag was one of Sal's favourite cakes, a pineapple cream, oozing sweet stickiness onto the bag. Next to it was a can, ice-cold, of cherry Coke and a packet of prawn cocktail crisps. Great! Sal stuffed it all down quickly as Mum rabbitted on.

'I always knew it wasn't you. Daft you may be, but not totally stupid. Anyway all's well that ends well, eh Sal?'

'Mmmm,' mumbled Sal, through the cake. Ending in pineapple cream wasn't too bad after all. It was great to feel believed in. She felt wonderful inside. Sal realised that Mum was sort of saying that she was sorry for not believing her. Well, she had been proved innocent. The rest of the family would have to be sorry as well!

The royal treatment continued until bedtime. Sal gave Boss and Grump a blow by blow account of what had happened in Mrs Preston's office.

'I'm sorry I didn't believe you,' said Grump, who was bored by now, with the third telling of the story.

'I'll tell you what,' Boss also wanted to escape. 'If you promise to be careful, you can borrow my personal stereo and "Hits Now" tape. Just tonight, mind you.'

Sal lay on her bed, in the usual position, the music dancing inside her head. This was great. I wonder how long this will last, she thought. Perhaps today would be a good time to ask Mum for some new curtains? Her thoughts were interrupted as Dad came into the room.

His huge presence dwarfed her as he sat heavily on the bed and turned towards her.

'So, it wasn't you after all, monkey?'

'No, Dad,' smiled Sal.

'That's good then. Here, I got you one of these. It's the real thing.'

Sal grasped the present eagerly. She'd wanted one for months. A bold blue and red striped cap with 'Truckers United' on it, just like Dad wore in his lorry. She put it on. It was miles too big and only stayed on her head at all because her snub nose stopped it from falling off.

'Oh, great!' She hurled herself at Dad who nearly squeezed the life out of her. He smelt sweaty and a whiff, like the infamous bad eggs, went up her nose.

'Cor, Dad, you stink!'

'Been shifting chemicals today. Better have my bath.' Dad heaved his bulk upright. 'Want to come to Bristol with me, tomorrow? Furniture this time.'

'Oh, yes.'

'Leave early, sixish.'

'Smashing!' When Dad had gone, Sal bounced up and down on the bed, the springs protesting loudly. A trucker's cap and a trip in the lorry! Dad had always said she was too young, before.

The trip lived up to all her expectations. They set off before anyone was awake and had breakfast in a transport café. It was fantastic. Bacon, sausage, egg, beans and wads of bread to wipe it up with, followed by scalding tea in a half-pint thick white pottery mug. Dad played his classical music, which was a bit of a bore, but let her put Radio One on sometimes.

Unloading took ages. Sal was so proud of Dad. He heaved settees and chairs around as if they were toys. His muscles bulged and rippled so much that you could see their outline under his shirt, which was by now wet with sweat.

On the journey home, Sal dozed off. She had made up her mind what she would do. Now she could answer that question grown-ups always asked 'And what do you want to be when you grow up?'

'A lorry driver,' she'd say, 'Like my dad.'

They'd save up and buy a lorry, a fleet of lorries, with 'Musgrove and Daughter' written right across the front. She'd eat lots so she could grow muscles. And she'd practise weight-lifting until she could throw heavy objects around as if they were paper.

Her dreams ended abruptly as the lorry drew to a halt outside their house. Stiffly she clambered down and went in.

'Hello, Sal. Had a nice day? Present for you. On your bed,' called Mum.

'Yes, great.' Sal ran upstairs, two at a time, her weariness gone. Another present? The curtains? Or duvet cover? But no. This was a plain brown box, all sellotaped up, and with Miss Sally Musgrove written on it.

Tearing the paper off, Sal unwrapped the biggest box of chocolates she had ever seen. It had sissy flowers on it but that didn't matter. She pulled the lid off and found her favourite. Caramel. Yummy. As the brown paper fell to the floor, Sal noticed a piece of white paper fluttering to join it. She grabbed it and unfolded it. By now on the third chocolate, hazelnut whirl, Sal sat back to read what was written.

Dear Sally. I am very sorry for letting you get into trouble. I know it was awful. I want to be your friend. Will you forgive me and be friends? Vicki.

Sal crumpled the note up and threw it across the room, where it bounced off the chest of drawers, before landing on the floor.

Absentmindedly helping herself to her seventh chocolate, Sal felt cross. Forgive her! Vicki! Be her friend! She must be joking. She'd never forgive her. Ever. Mind you, she'd keep the chocolates. No point wasting them. Sal got up and retrieved the note. She smoothed it out on her lap and re-read it. Just for a minute something inside her said, go on, Sal, forgive her, be friends. But no, she couldn't. What would the others think?

Looking at the note, Sal had an idea. Two could play at this game. Two people could write notes. She could get her own back on Vicki and get her out of the gang at the same time. Tomorrow she would put her plan into action.

14

'Sal, are you going to be in there all morning?'

'No, Mum, I'm practising my writing. For school.'
The first bit was true, anyway. Sal's bed was littered
with scraps of paper, covered in smudges and crossings-
out. Trying to write like other people was harder than
she had imagined. The one from Cowboy was all right.
His big uphill scrawl was fairly easy to copy. And maybe
this one would do for Tag's. It was virtually unreadable,
the words squashed together in the smallest possible
space. Miss Winter was always telling Tag that she
needed a magnifying glass to decipher his work.

Narrinder's was the hardest. Her writing was just like
her, neat and tidy. At the fourth attempt, Sal gave up.
It would have to do. Quickly she scribbled her own note
and put all four letters into different coloured envelopes.
Mum wouldn't notice for weeks that her beautifully
boxed letter writing set had been raided. Sal ran
downstairs.

'Where are you off to, Sal? There's work to be done,'
called Mum, who was in the throes of preparing Sunday
dinner.

'A walk. Won't be long.'

'It's pouring. You'll get soaked.'

Sal ignored her. 'Tara. Back soon.'

In ten minutes she was outside the correct house. It
stared blankly at her, the heavily net-curtained windows

giving nothing away. Sal opened the wrought iron gate, noticing the pattern of a peacock on it, and let it clang shut. Quickly she ran up the short gravel path. She rammed the letters into the brass letter box and turned and ran. Her heart was beating fast, and it wasn't just from the running. Perhaps it had not been such a good idea, after all. Then she thought of how she had been so unfairly treated.

'Serve her right,' she said out loud, slowing her running into a gentle jog. She noticed, for the first time, that she was dripping wet. Little rivulets streamed down the back of her neck. Her denim jeans had stuck to her legs where the rain had poured off her anorak. Sal felt cold and clammy and was glad to reach the warm haven of home.

'I told you you'd be drenched,' commented Mum. 'Now, have a quick bath. You'll catch your death of cold.'

As Sal lay in the steaming water, she felt pleased with herself. It's not exactly a trick, she thought, but it's pretty good. I wonder what she'll think.

Sal soon found out the next day at school. Vicki had to sit at the dreaded desk right by the teacher. Her moon shaped face looked all blotched and red, as if she had had a good cry.

At break, Vicki went over to Brian and the two of them spent all their time as far away from the gang as possible.

Rats, thought Sal, I should have done one from Brian as well. Forgot all about him. Mind you, his spelling was ace and doing four letters had taken her hours.

'What's up with those two?' asked Tag, pointing to the dejected pair who were slowly walking around the perimeter of the playground.

'Look like animals at the zoo,' said Cowboy. 'You know, the ones that just walk up and down their cages all day.'

'Always said she was an elephant,' Sal joined in.

'And Brian must be a giraffe.'

'No, he's too little. More like a . . . a hyena, with his hair sticking up.'

'Let's go and see what's up with them,' Narrinder started towards them but Sal grabbed her arm and held her back.

'No. Leave them alone. We're better off without them.' Sal sounded determined. 'If they wanted to join us, they would have done.'

The gang gave up and went back to sorting out their secret codes. Sal felt great. Her plan had worked. Not only had she got her own back on Vicki, but she had also got the gang for herself. This was much better.

However it was only much better until the next morning.

'Sally,' said Miss Winter sternly. 'I want to see you, straight after lunch. Here.'

The look on Miss Winter's face stopped Sal from asking any questions. So at 12:21 by Boss's digital watch, which she had borrowed again without asking, Sal found herself once more in conversation with Miss Winter. The teacher took no time at all to come to the point.

'Sally, I'm ashamed of you. Ashamed. After all we did, too, to sort out the accident business.'

What now? thought Sal, who knew that she had not done any tricks at school for weeks.

'You needn't pretend to be puzzled,' continued Miss Winter. 'It was a despicable trick to write these,' and she placed the four notes slowly and deliberately on the table.

How on earth had Miss found them? Sal went bright red with embarrassment. Had Vicki brought them to school? Sensing the question, Miss Winter carried on.

'Mrs Simpkins, Vicki's mother, telephoned the school

yesterday. So I went to see her.'

'Went to see her?' Sal voiced her puzzlement. Parents always went to teachers, not the other way around.

'Well, I could hardly expect her to get up the steps here in her wheelchair.'

Sal was astonished. Wheelchair? That was why she had never seen Mrs Simpkins. How awful to have a mum in a wheelchair.

'She told me that Vicki was very upset at the letters from four of her classmates and asked if I could do anything about it. When I read the letters, I realised that I could . . . so I am.'

Sal just stared at her. If only she had known about Vicki's mum, she might have been nicer to her.

'Honestly, Sal, as a forger you are hopeless. Every letter reads the same. "Vicki Simpkins, we don't want you in our club any more. You can get lost," signed Cowboy, or Tag or Sal or Narrinder.'

'How did you know it was me?' asked Sal, not bothering to deny it.

'Well, apart from the fact that you are the only one in the class that always writes "are" not "our", and who spells "signed" as "synd", you did leave one rather obvious clue. Look.'

Sal stared at where Miss Winter was pointing. She ran her finger unbelievingly across the paper. You could feel it clearly. Her address, not printed but embossed into the posh writing paper. Her mind flashed back to when Mum had asked Grandma Musgrove when she would ever need to use such smart writing paper. Sal hadn't even noticed it on Sunday, so intent was she to get the writing done.

'18, Victoria Terrace, Armbridge . . . need I go on?'

'No, Miss,' Sal hung her head, shamefully.

'Why did you do it?'

'I had to get my own back. For what she had done.

It wasn't fair.'

'And this is fair?'

There was a long silence. Sal felt very uncomfortable and wondered what was coming next.

'Sally, Mrs Preston told you about forgiving and forgetting, didn't she?'

Sal nodded.

'You haven't taken much notice of it, have you?' Sal shook her head. 'Why do you think we should forgive?'

'Dunno,' Sal squirmed in her seat.

'Well, I'll tell you why. First, it causes a lot of trouble if we don't; second, we feel a lot better inside; and thirdly, it is the right thing to do. Do you remember how I forgave you when I thought it was your fault I'd hurt my head?'

'Yes, Miss.'

'Why do you think I did that?'

'To be nice, Miss.'

'Sort of. You see, Sal, I wanted to forgive you because I believe that's what God wanted me to do. Remember when we did the Easter story, we talked about Jesus dying for us, because he loved us, and why else?'

Sal racked her brains. 'To forgive us,' she said eventually.

'That's right. Jesus forgives us for the wrong things we have done, and in turn we should forgive other people.'

'But I don't really want to forgive Vicki,' said Sal.

'I can understand that. I want you to go away and think about things, Sally. It might help you to remember that bit in the Lord's prayer that we say most days, you know, forgive us as we forgive others.'

Miss Winter stood up and Sal felt relieved that the session was nearly over.

'And, Sal, I want you to apologise to Vicki. To say sorry. Will you do that?'

Sal grunted by way of reply and drifted off out to the

playground. She did not want to be with her friends just now. She wanted to be on her own. To think. Finding herself near the kitchen door, she leaned hard on an enormous grey dustbin. It smelt of cabbage and gravy, potatoes and solid yellow custard. Not that Sal minded. At least she was on her own here.

There were no two ways about it. She would have to forgive Vicki. But it was so hard. I know, she thought, I'll tell God about it. This forgiveness thing sounded like it was his idea in the first place. Perhaps it was hard for him to forgive people. It must have been awfully hard for Jesus. After all, he had had to die! At least she hadn't got to do that.

I'll talk to him again, she thought. I'll say it out loud, just to make sure he can hear.

Sal shut her eyes tight, like they were supposed to do in Assembly. 'It's me, God, Sally Musgrove, 18, Victoria Terrace,' she paused. 'I need some help. I've got to forgive Vicki, but it's hard. I think it was hard for you as well, so I expect that you know what I mean. I've just thought, I'd better say sorry to you too. I am sorry, really. I don't want to be nasty to Vicki. Please will you "forgive us our sins as we forgive everyone who does us wrong." ' Sal finished with the words from the Lord's prayer.

'Right, God,' she said. 'It's up to you and me now. Let's go,' and Sal strode purposefully from her place by the dustbins, into the playground. This was it. She took three deep breaths, crossed her fingers hidden deep in her anorak pockets, and set off towards her. Towards Vicki.

15

'Vicki, can I talk to you?' Sal looked pointedly at Brian, who was with her. 'On your own.' Brian scuttled off, over towards the rest of the gang, who, Sal was sure, were staring at her.

'Vicki,' she began, gazing into the distance, as though the sight of the back end of Allsop's factory fascinated her. 'Vicki, I've, er, I want to . . . um, want to . . . say I'm sorry. I was horrible to you for ages. It was me who sent the notes, not the others. I am sorry. Will you forgive me. Be my friend?'

Sal did not dare to look at Vicki. The silence went on for what seemed like eternity. Then Vicki spoke softly, so that Sal had to look at her to hear her words properly.

'I'm sorry, too. I was really glad when everyone thought it was you, you know, with the chair. I hated you then.'

'I hated you, too.'

'Well, we'll be friends now.' At Vicki's words, Sal heaved a sigh of relief. It hadn't been that bad after all. Thanks God, she thought, looking up into the sky. She felt like she could float across the playground. A little bubble of happiness started to grow from deep inside her until she thought that she would burst with joy. A genuine smile lit up her face.

'Come on, Vicki, let's join the gang.' Sal put her arm around her and then curiosity got the better of her.

'Why's your mum in a wheelchair?'

Vicki did not seem to mind the question. 'She's got this muscle disease. Now her legs don't work properly. That's why we came here. To live at Grandma and Grandpa's. They're at home when Dad's at work, in case Mum needs help.'

Sal was thoughtful. Imagine her own mum, in a wheelchair. How would they all manage?

'Where have you been all break?' asked Narrinder.

'Oh, nowhere,' Sal did not want to talk about what had happened. 'Anyway, Vicki and Brian are back in the gang. Okay?'

'Always was,' muttered Tag.

'Can we really come to your house?' asked Cowboy, who was still itching to explore its secret interior.

'Of course. I'll ask Mum when,' replied Vicki.

'We can't,' interrupted Sal, 'not with your mum.'

'Don't be stupid. She's not ill, just stuck in a wheelchair,' Vicki explained. 'She won't mind.'

And so it was arranged that the gang, all six of them, would meet at Vicki's house that Saturday afternoon. The plan was to sort out details for the club. Things like membership rules, how much to pay, what to call themselves, and codes that they could actually remember, had to be decided upon.

However, unknown to Sal, there was another plan afoot and Saturday afternoon would hold more surprises than she had bargained for.

The five children arrived promptly at two o'clock to be greeted by Vicki. In honour of the occasion, Sal was wearing her best jeans, the ones without holes, an oversized sweatshirt that said 'Olympics' on it, and her 'Trucker's United' cap.

They were not disappointed in their visit. The house was enormous. The dark oak panelled hallway was as big as Sal's living room, and a stuffed stag's head seemed to be watching them. The lounge was brighter, with old-fashioned heavy furniture in it. Mrs Simpkins was sitting in there. Sal felt a bit strange but she need not have. Mrs Simpkins looked younger than her own mum. Her wavy brown hair curled up on her shoulders and she was wearing a beautiful multi-coloured patchwork jumper. Her weak legs looked fine in grey silky trousers. In fact there was nothing to be scared of here.

Vicki introduced them all.

'So you're Sal,' said Mrs Simpkins. 'Heard a lot about you.'

Sal gulped. Oh, no, not another lecture. She wished that she had not come.

'Sounds like you should all have fun together.' Vicki's mum's grey eyes twinkled and she broke into a smile. It was okay. 'Now off you go and play.'

'Still thinks I'm a baby,' said Vicki, leading the way up the carved curving staircase into a long room that ran the length of the house. 'This is my room.'

It was superb. There were two beds covered with bright yellow duvets which were echoed in the curtains. The whole of one wall was covered in a picture. A giant rainbow arched for its full length and underneath hills, trees, rivers and villages were picked out in great detail.

'It's fantastic,' said Tag. 'Who did it?'

'Mum.'

'Your mum? How?'

'It was her job, before she was ill. Painting murals. Now she only does a few. Dad makes up this scaffold thing, so she can sit in her chair and reach the high bits.' Vicki did not seem to think there was anything strange in this. 'Come on, let's get these codes sorted out.'

In the end they decided that the best code was the easiest. All you had to do was to write your message backwards.

'Let's try it out,' said Sal.

'Okay,' Vicki was grinning for some reason. 'You go over there,' she said pointing to her bed, 'and we'll write you a message, that you've got to do.'

There was some whispering and giggling. Vicki left the room briefly and returned.

'Right, Sal, off you go.'

'Where?'

'Just follow the code. Here.' Vicki passed her a piece of paper. Sal noticed that Cowboy was being insane, rolling on one of the beds, with his fists stuffed into his mouth.

She looked at the paper. 'Shut eyes your with right the on door second the through in straight walk and, left turn, door the of out go.' Sal read it aloud.

'It's easy.'

'Well, go on, do it,' said Tag.

Sal shrugged her shoulders. If it amused them, she would follow the instructions.

It amused them all right! Especially when Sal went through the second door on the right. The light cardboard box toppled off the top of the door and scattered its varied contents over her, before resting gracefully over her shoulders.

'Hey, what the heck is going on!' came a muffled voice.

Cowboy was totally hysterical, while Narrinder chuckled to Vicki. 'It worked. A real beaut!'

Brian began, 'It was my idea . . .' when Sal stumbled and fell over a rug. Pulling the box from off her head she glared at the others. How dare they? Playing a trick on her! Then she started to laugh. She was covered in curly beige wood shavings, crunched up pieces of white polystyrene out of some packaging, the remains of last year's Christmas paper chains and cornflakes.

'Ah, delicious,' she said, retrieving a handful of cornflakes and stuffing them in her mouth. 'Where's the milk?' and Sal aimed a fistful of mess at the others.

They had a wonderful fight. Bits of polystyrene floated through the air and danced with the shavings, until the room and the gang were covered in the glorious mix, and all the cornflakes were crushed to smithereens beneath their feet. Puffed out with laughing, they sat down.

'Grief, what a mess!'

'Your mum will do her nut.'

'No, she knows,' replied Vicki.

'Knows?'

'Course. She said we could do it.'

Sal was dumb-struck. Fancy having a mum who let you do crazy things. They'd come here as much as possible.

'Got to vac up, though,' said Vicki, and they all set too. It took longer than they thought because Narrinder put the hose in the wrong end of the vacuum cleaner. And so a pile of dust was added to the general chaos first.

As they sat eating tea, Sal was thinking, actually this garlic bread was not bad. You could breathe all over people and pretend to be a dragon. It was strange really, to have had a trick played on her. She could understand a bit better now why the family had got mad at her so often. Still she had been able to laugh about it and it had been brill fun.

'You should have been there, Mum,' said Vicki, handing round the biggest stickiest doughnuts Sal had ever seen.

'Didn't want you left out, eh, Sal,' said Tag.

'Now that you've had a trick played on you, Miss Musgrove,' Narrinder was pretending to be a reporter complete with microphone, 'Do tell the viewers what it feels like.'

Sal put on a posh voice and attempted to flutter her

eyelashes, but looked as if she had developed a bad case of the twitches.

'Since you've asked,' she began. 'At first it was awful, but then it was brill. We'll have to think up some more tricks.'

'Oh, no!' chorused five voices.

'Give it a break.'

'Not at school, please.'

Sal was determined to have the last word. 'I'll tell you what, when we do the next trick, we'll *all* do it. Together.'

Some other Tiger books which you might like to read . . .

Operation Sandy

Cathie Bartlam

Mick is very fond of Sandy, who is being trained as a guide dog by his friend's family. He plans Operation Sandy and runs away with the dog. Afterwards he begins to understand why Sandy could never be his dog.

The Project

Gail Vinall

John and Sarah are reluctant to share their project on the coastguard station with Jamie, the new boy in their class. He is not very friendly and they sense that he is trying to hide something. When they find out the truth, they are able to work on the project and they solve another mystery together.

Defenders of the Valley

Pat Coleman

Developers want to buy Viking Farm but Peter's uncle refuses to sell. Then some sheep are stolen and things disappear from the nearby castle too. Peter, Seb, Fiona and Mike discover a link and fight back to save the valley. Another story about the characters in *Smugglers' Cove*.

Smugglers' Cove

Pat Coleman

Seb and Fiona are spending their summer holidays at their grandmother's house. They make friends with Mike and Peter and together go exploring the caves along the coast. Mike and Peter have heard stories of smugglers in bygone days and want to find the cave they used. After a frightening incident on the beach they discover that Peter has more than his fair share of problems and they determine to help him find a way round them.

The Fen Street Flyer
Graham Jones
Another amusing story about Paul, Oliver, Richard, Eddie and the other characters in *The Bike*. As a joke, Paul and Oliver are nominated to take part in a talent contest for a TV show. Their performance is a disaster but as a result the organisers discover the Fen Street Rock Calypso band and invite them on the show. Then their instruments are stolen just before the show. Paul decides to do some investigating, starting with Eddie.

The Inca Trail
Vivien Whitfield
A collection of stories about children in Peru whose lives are very different from ours. Roberto is a shepherd up in the mountains who wants to get away to the town. Lisbet lives in a shanty town and has never seen the sea until she goes to camp. Luis is a guide to the tourists who come to visit the Inca ruins.

The Shell Box
Carol Oldham
It is the summer holidays and Laura and Tim are looking forward to a seaside holiday with their cousins, Mark and Alice. Then Theresa is fostered with Laura's family and Laura becomes very possessive of her, resenting Mark's attempts to be friendly to

Theresa and imagining he is trying to get her away from Laura. When Theresa is lost one day, Mark gets the blame and he decides to make a shell box for Theresa to show he is sorry. Laura takes the box before he can give it to Theresa and hides it. Then things really start to go wrong.